The Black God's Drums

THE BLACK GOD'S DRUMS

P. DJÈLÍ CLARK

A TOM DOHERTY ASSOCIATES BOOK

NEW YORK

THE BLACK GOD'S DRUMS

Cover art by Chris McGrath
Cover design by Christine Foltzer

Edited by Diana M. Pho

A Tor.com Book
Published by Tom Doherty Associates
175 Fifth Avenue
New York, NY 10010

www.tor.com

Tor® is a registered trademark of
Macmillan Publishing Group, LLC.

ISBN 978-1-250-29471-5 (trade paperback)
ISBN 978-1-250-29470-8 (ebook)

First Edition: August 2018

To those who survived the crossing,
and who carried their Black gods with them.

"I have avenged America."
—Jean-Jacques (JanJak) Dessalines

The night in New Orleans always got something going on, ma maman used to say—like this city don't know how to sleep. You want a good look, take the cable-elevator to the top of one of Les Grand Murs, where airships dock on the hour. Them giant iron walls ring the whole Big Miss on either side. Up here you can see New Algiers on the West Bank, its building yards all choked in factory smoke and workmen scurrying round the bones of new-built vessels like ants. Turn around and there's the downtown wards lit up with gas lamps like glittering stars. You can make out the other wall in the east over at Lake Borgne, and a fourth one like a crescent moon up north round Swamp Pontchartrain—what most folk call La Ville Morte, the Dead City.

Les Grand Murs were built by Dutchmen to protect against the storms that come every year. Not the regular hurricanes neither, but them tempêtes noires that turn the skies into night for a whole week. I was born in one of the big ones some thirteen years back in 1871. The walls held in the Big Miss but the rain and winds almost drowned the city anyway, filling it up like a bowl. Ma maman pushed me out her belly in that storm, clinging to a big sweet gum tree in the middle of thunder and lightning. She said I was Oya's child—the goddess of storms, life, death, and rebirth, who came over with her great-grandmaman from Lafrik, and who runs strong in our blood. Ma maman said that's why I take to high places so, looking to ride Oya's wind.

Les Grand Murs is where I call home these days. It's not the finest accommodations: drafty on winter nights and so hot in the summer all you do is lay about in your own sweat. But lots of street kids set up for themselves up here. Better than getting swept into workhouse orphanages or being conscripted to steal for a Thieving Boss.

Me, I marked out a prime spot: an alcove just some ways off from one of the main airship mooring masts. That's where the gangplanks are laid down for disembarking passengers heading into the city. Concealed in my alcove, I can see them all: in every colour and shade, in every sort of dress, talking in more languages than I can count, their voices competing with the rattle of dirigible engines and the hum of ship propellers. It always gets me to thinking on how there's a whole world out there, full of all kinds of people. One day, I dream, I'm going to get on one of those airships. I'll sail away from this city into the clouds and visit all the places there are to visit, and see all the people there are to see. Of course, watching from my alcove is also good for marking out folk too careless with their purses, luggage, and anything else for the taking. Because in New Orleans, you can't survive on just dreams.

My eyes latch onto a little dandy-looking man in a rusty plaid suit, with slicked-back shiny brown hair and a curly moustache. He got a tight grip on his bags, but there's a golden pocket watch dangling on a chain at his side. A clear invitation if I ever seen one. Somebody's bound to snatch it sooner or later—might as well be me.

I'm about to set out to follow him when the world suddenly slows. The air, sounds, everything. It's like somebody grabbed hold of time and stretched her out at both ends. I turn, slow-like, to look out from the wall as a monstrous moon begins to rise into the sky. No, not a moon, I realize in fright—a skull! A great big bone white skull that fills up the night. It pushes itself up past the horizon to cast a shadow over the city underneath, where the gaslights snuff out one by one. I gape at that horrible face, stripped clean of skin or flesh, that stares back with deep empty black sockets and a grin of bared teeth. It's all I can do not to fall to my knees.

"Not real!" I whisper, shutting my eyes to make the apparition go away. I count to ten in my head, whispering all the while: "Not real! Not real! Not real!"

When I open my eyes again, the skull moon is gone. Time has caught up to normal too—the sounds of the night returning in a rush. And the city is there, spread out again: breathing, shining and alive. I release a breath. This was all Oya's doing, I know. The goddess has strange ways of talking. Not the first time I've been sent one of her visions—though never anything so strong. Never anything that felt so real. They're what folk call premonitions: warnings of things about to happen or things soon to come. Most times I can figure them out quick. But a giant skull moon? I got no damn idea what that's supposed to mean.

"You could just talk to me plain," I mutter in irritation. But Oya doesn't answer. She's already humming a song that whistles in my ears. It's about her mother Yemoja leading some lost fishermen to shore. The moon is Yemoja's domain, after all. Giving up, I turn back, hoping to find my mark again—but instead, I'm startled by the sound of footsteps.

My whole body goes still. Not just footsteps but boots, by the way they fall heavy. More than one pair too. I curse at my bad luck, ducking back down into my alcove. I chose this spot special, because it's some ways off from the usual paths people take—just near enough for me to see them, but far enough to keep out of their way. No one ever comes this far out, to this part of the wall. But those steps are getting closer, heading right for me! Cursing my luck twice again, I scramble back to huddle into a far corner of the alcove, where the shadows fall deep. I'm small enough to curl into a ball if I draw my knees up under me. And if I go real still, I might escape without being seen. I might.

I'm expecting constables. Rare to see any of them up here, but could be the city's decided to do a sweep for one reason or the other. Maddi grá coming up, and they like to make everything look respectable to visitors—respectable for New Orleans, anyway. Maybe someone's complained about all the street kids up here picking pockets. Or worse yet, could be the city's workhouses and factories need more small hands to run their machines—machines that seem to delight in stealing fingers. I grit my teeth and ball up my fists as if trying to protect my own fingers, not daring to breathe. Damn sure ain't going to end up in one of those places.

But the figures that enter my alcove aren't constables. They're men, though, about five of them. I can't make them out in the dark, but by their height and the way they walk they have to be men. They're not wearing the telltale blue uniforms of constables though, with the upside-down gold crescent and five-pointed star stitched on their shoulders. These men are wearing dull faded gray uniforms that almost blend into the dark. Their jackets got patches on the front that I recognize right off:

white stars in a blue cross like an X over a bed of red, the letters CSA stitched underneath. The brisk twangs that roll off their tongues are Southern, but like those uniforms, certainly nothing made in New Orleans.

"Alright then," one of them says. "You can get us what we want?"

"Deal already set up, Capitaine," another voice answers, real casual-like. This one's a Cajun. I'd recognize that bayou accent anywhere. I lift my chin off my knees to risk a peek from under the lid of my cap. The one talking that Cajun talk ain't got on a uniform. He's wearing some old brown pants and a red shirt with suspenders. I still can't make out any faces, but can see a mop of white hair on his head almost down to his shoulders. "Dat scientist be here next day, on a morning airship from Haiti. Gonna see to meeting him myself."

My ears perk up at that. A Haitian scientist? Meeting with these men?

"How long we have to wait?" a third voice asks. This one's impatient, almost whining. "Captain, we don't need all this fuss. I say we just snatch him when he gets here. Put him on our ship and fly off. Have him in Charleston in no time."

The Cajun makes a tsking sound. "Ma Lay! Do dat, brudda, and you get de constables involved. Dey gonna cost you mo dan I do. Not how we do tings down here, no."

"Seems all you folk *do* in this city is drink and gamble and eat," the third voice sneers.

The Cajun chuckles. "We like to pass a good time. Make music and babies too."

The first voice, the one both men called Captain, steps in then. Sounds like he's trying to keep things from boiling over. I glance to those black-booted feet, realizing I hadn't pulled my sleeping blanket into the corner with me. That was careless. But nothing I can do about it now. My heart beats faster, hoping none of them steps on it or bothers to look down.

"So after this scientist gets here," the captain is saying, "then what?"

"When he get settled, I set up de meeting between the two of you," the Cajun answers. There's a pause. "You got what he coming all dis way to get? You don't deliver, he might run."

"We got his jewel, alright," the third voice says in his usual sneer.

The Cajun claps, and I imagine him smiling. "Den it should work out fine." He extends a hand and the captain offers over a thick wad of something. The unmistakable beautiful sound of crisp bills being counted fills up my alcove.

"You'll get the rest when we see this scientist—and his invention," the captain states.

"Wi, Capitaine," the Cajun replies. "You give him his jewel and he gonna hand over dat ting you want." He stops his counting and leans in close. "De Black God's Drums. Maybe you boys able to win dis war yet, yeah."

The captain dips his head in a nod before answering. "Maybe."

There's some more talk. Nothing important from what I can tell. Just the questions and assurances of men who don't trust each other and who up to no good. But I'm only half-listening by now. My mind is on the words the Cajun said: the Black God's Drums. With a Haitian scientist involved, that can only mean one thing. And if I'm right, that's big. Bigger than any marks I was going to pinch tonight. This is information that's gonna be valuable to somebody. I just need to figure out who'll pay the highest price. Long after the men leave my alcove, I sit there thinking hard in the dark as Oya hums in my head.

~

Two nights later, it's all hustle and bustle the Sunday before the Maddi grá. Most times like now I'd be mixed up in all that tumult, getting ready to strut and sashay with the best of them. But not tonight. Tonight, I got a meeting. And some information to sell—or trade.

I cut through the Quarter, to get a glimpse of some of

the action—and mostly to do some light pocket-picking along the way. I'm small enough not to get noticed. Just a bit of Oya's wind is more than ample to send wallets or bills flying. The goddess disapproves of my using her gift this way, and tells me as much, tickling the way she do in my head. But she also understands I got to keep my belly full, and lets me do as I need. Makes her grumble some, but I don't pay her no mind.

I change my route when I catch sight of some Bakers though. Their faces are powdered with flour to match their white jackets and pants; only bit of colour on them are the blood red kerchiefs around their necks and the rouge on their cheeks. They swagger about, thumbing the handles of flat wooden paddles fitted into belts at their waists: whole lot of them just itching for a fight. The Guildes of New Orleans are out strong tonight—Bakers, Boilermakers, Mechanics, you name it—and touchy about their territory. Then again, when ain't they? There'll be some blood flowing before the dawn come, you just watch. And that kind of trouble I can do without.

It's as I'm trying to duck away from them that I end up running into someone. Usually Oya's gift lets me move light on my feet, so that I slip around and about other people like a passing breeze. But this time it don't work for some reason. I hit the other person head-on, so hard it sends me bouncing off him to fall right on my backside.

Blinking, I look up to find a tall skinny man in a tight black suit, like what the morticians who run the city's best funeral parlors wear. When I see his face, I almost try to scramble back and away. It's a skull, bone white and grinning like the one in my vision! Only this isn't no phantom. You don't bounce off phantoms, I tell myself, trying to be sensible. Looking closer, I realize his face is really a mask—white bones painted on black cloth.

I breathe easier, feeling kind of foolish. It's a little early for masking, true. But no accounting for when some folk decide to start their Maddi grá. The man tilts his head to the side to peer down at me, with blue eyes like chipped bits of ice.

"Best watch where you going, cher," he scolds playfully, stressing that last word as he takes in my clothing. He extends a suntanned hand towards me, with long spidery fingers and red tattoos painted on the knuckles. I'm about to accept his help when Oya hisses loud in my head. Dammit! It hurts! It sounds like a rising wind in a fierce storm moving through trees, or blasting down a corridor between buildings. I snatch my hand back, just to make it stop. Something in those icy eyes turns hot for a moment, but the man just drops his hand to his side and laughs—a cackle coming from behind that grinning skull that raises up bumps on my skin.

"Suit yourself den, cher." He shrugs. Moving around

me where I still sit, he makes his way down the street.
He don't walk, though. Instead, he does a funny little soft
shuffling dance with his feet while mouthing the words
to some tune I never heard before:

> *"Remember New Orleans I say,*
> *Where Jackson show'd them Yankee play,*
> *And beat them off and gain'd the day,*
> *And then we heard the people say*
> *Huzza! for Gen'ral Jackson!"*

I shake my head. An unusual fellow, no doubting it.
Probably why Oya took a disliking to him. She can be
particular like that. But being strange ain't no crime. Not
in New Orleans. Could be he got something to do with
the vision she sent me two days back. Or she think he
do. Only, he ain't the first or last skeleton I'm gonna see
at Maddi grá. Can't go off chasing after every one just to
figure out what's got her so prickly. My hands full as it is.
Picking myself up, I spare one last glance for the odd man
then turn and set out again on my business.

By the time I reach Madamesville I can hear the bells
at Saint Louis tolling the hour. I stop once to let a mudbug scuttle down Robertson. Its six iron legs clang heavy
on the cobblestones while curving pipes on its back
belch out black smoke, looking like some big old crawfish

what crawled out the bayou. The constable driving the thing squints my way through a pair of bronze goggles. He looks me over once, then turns back in his cushioned seat to continue his rounds without stopping. No time for a street rat like me when there'll be all kinds of mayhem out tonight. I cross behind him and arrive at my destination.

Shá Rouj isn't the best bordello in Madamesville, certainly nothing like the big mansions up on Basin Street. But it ain't one of the tucked away 50-cent joints either, that some say got more rats than ladies. Madame Diouf keeps it nice, with bright cherry red paint and white shutters, all behind fancy iron railings that twist and curve into ivies. A great big cat's head, painted black in a red top hat and a gold monocle, grins down at me from the roof and winks a lazy mechanical eye. I tip my cap and wink back for luck before stepping through the front door.

The stink of cigars and too-sweet perfume hits me right off and I wrinkle my nose at the mix. The house is full tonight, more than usual. There's men sitting on rose-coloured sofas and chairs or standing about—drinking whiskey and rum, keeping up a loud chatter that rolls and echoes about the room. The women on their laps don't wear much beyond stockings, frills, and lace corsets, but their painted faces are always smiling. I see one tug her ear and a server man in a white wig, bright gold breeches, and a long fancy red coat—with tails even—rushes to keep everybody's cups full.

Shá Rouj was built to look like free New Orleans. It lets in men of any colour and offers women just the same—big Dutch gals, scarlet-haired Irish, dark senoritas, midnight-black Senegalese. And like New Orleans, Shá Rouj is neutral territory. Where else can you find Frenchie corsairs making all nice with British Jack Tars? There's Prussians, New Mexicans, Gran Columbians—even some Kalifornians, in their peculiar Russian dress. I count about a dozen black men, all showy and boisterous. Haitians by the looks of it, all gussied up in blue and red uniforms.

I pick through the crowd, searching for one face in particular. My eyes fix instead on some men sitting in a corner and drinking quietly—all in familiar dull faded gray uniforms with the Southern Cross battle flag on their sleeves, the words CSA inscribed beneath in red stitching. Confederate States soldiers. Air Force, by the badges on their shoulders. My heart thumps as I wonder if they're the same ones from the other night in my alcove. Pretty certain no one saw me. But still, I walk the other way, keeping a good bit of distance between us. Funny to find Confederates in here anyway, what with all this open miscegenation. They keep to themselves, their eyes wandering every now and again to a knot of loud-talking officers in unmistakable dark Union blue—New York Bowery Boys by those rough accents and their sheer bawdiness. Any other day these allies and enemies might be at each other's throats. But tonight they share the same space and mind their manners. Because this is New Orleans—one of the few nonaligned territories in the now broken United States.

New Orleans been free now going on more than two decades—ever since the slave uprising in that first year of the war. Caught the Confederates by surprise. They got so scared, they let the Free Coloured militias join up to help put it down. Only the militias switched over to the slaves and both of them took the city. After that, Union ships and troops came in and got into one big batay with the Confederates. Was them two that burned Old Algiers. New Orleans hunkered down and waited it out. Finally, the Haitians and Brits and Frenchies sent their airships to stop the fighting. Truce was signed making New Orleans a neutral and open port.

Free Coloured men tried to cheat the slaves soon after, hoping to put them back on the plantations. But when it looked like another uprising was brewing, they passed emancipation real quick. A council runs New Orleans today, made up of ex-slaves, mulattoes and white business folk. Brits, Frenchies, and Haitians patrol our harbors and skies to keep the peace. Confederates and the Union ain't had a big tussle in fifteen years—not since the Armistice of Third Antietam. But if that war ever starts back up, New Orleans gonna find herself right in the middle of it again. Folk say that's why we live every day chasing the good times. Because you never know when the bad might come.

"Goad a'michty!" I look up to find a round splotchy-faced Scotsman in a milk-white suit pointing a thick forefinger at me. Two plump octoroons hang off his arms, with piled-up hair and red crescent moons on their cheeks, wearing nothing but frilly pink corsets and black striped stockings. "Lad's too young to be here, d'ye think?" he protests to no one in particular.

"Not a lad," I mutter, pulling off my cap to reveal a thick halo of black hair and a nut-brown face.

The Scotsman's eyes widen then narrow hungrily. Rum and wine got his face as ruddy as his side whiskers. "Hou much for the wee one?" he asks aloud. I think he's joking. Maybe. Oya don't. There's a rumbling thunder in my ear. She's protective like that.

"Too young for you, sir," another voice puts in sternly. "And not for sale."

I turn to find a woman striding down a set of stairs towards us, her hand lightly trailing the wooden bannister.

She'd be tall even without the evening heels, with black skin and hair turned a dark smoky gray. Her face is striking, as beautiful as a painting I once seen of the Queen of Sheba. She moves like she's walking on water, the roomy skirts of her ruffled blue dress swishing about her legs in waves. In my head Oya's anger settles, and she starts up another song about Yemoja—who tricked her from her throne under the sea.

"Guid eenin Madame Diouf," the Scotsman greets her, stumbling into a bow that almost topples him. "I meant no offense."

The proprietor of Shá Rouj blinks once before smiling. I'm always envious when I look into those black eyes, like what I imagine the deepest part of the sea must look like. Mine are murky as swamp water, a plain muddy brown.

"No offense taken, sir," she croons in her Afrikin accent. "Have you tried the special whiskey I've had shipped in? From a distillery in your native country. A place called Orkney? Compliments of the house for you, sir." The Scotsman's face lights up and he begins to babble on excitedly about having family from this Orkney, forgetting I'm even there. Madame Diouf listens politely, then at her nod the Scotsman is pulled away by his escorts, their hips swaying with loose flesh that seems to push him along between them. She promptly turns her attention to me, showing an appraising eye. "Little creeping vine. What brings you here tonight?"

"It's just Creeper, Madame Diouf," I respond.

The older woman grimaces. "Mondjé! I prefer the name your mother gave you, *Jacqueline*." She runs her fingers through my unkempt hair and tugs at the too-big brown coat on my small frame. Oya scowls as deep as I do. We don't like being fidgeted with. "This hair could use braiding! And what is all this? Where did you get those ridiculous trousers? Do you want to be mistaken for a boy?"

I pull away, putting my cap back on and tucking my hair beneath. "On the streets, better people make that mistake."

Madame Diouf puts on a severe frown. Damn Afrikin. Even that's beautiful. "You aren't out there running with those Guildes, are you?" she asks. "Gangs of thieves and worse!"

"I don't have nothing to do with any Guildes," I retort, somewhat offended. As if I'd take on dressing up like one of those clowns.

Madame Diouf looks me over skeptically. Then that beautiful face softens. She leans down, smelling sweet like honey and jasmine. I get dizzy in the haze of her. "You have no need to stay on the street, Jacqueline," she reminds. "Your mother was like my own daughter. Enough schools in the city to take you in."

"Tried that already," I shoot back. "Those girls hold their noses around a 'pitènn's daughter.'"

Madame Diouf stands up and lets out a string of curses in her mix of Creole and Afrikin talk. It's impressive enough to raise my eyebrows. "What nerve!" she huffs. "Mothers just two steps out of chains and they're putting on airs!" She pats my head again, then runs the back of her long fingers across my cheek. "Well, I'll have one of the girls set up a bath for you. Have them braid your hair up at least, yes? Get some proper clothes on you too. And stay and take some food. To maig' comme coucou! Put some fat on those bones!"

By the time I'm led to a kitchen table in the back of the house, I been freshly soaped, scrubbed and washed, and had my hair tied down in thick braids. Kept my own clothes, though. No matter what Madame Diouf think, dresses don't do me no good on the street. I settle down into a chair and busy myself licking grease off my fingers as I pull meat from a bit of fried pork. Oya's disappointed there's no hen. I stay away from the roast mutton, though, which the goddess abhors. Eat that and she'll have me bringing it back up half the night.

From where I sit I can see everything in the main room. I watch all the cavorting and carrying on as the women of Shá Rouj smile, wink, laugh, and wiggle every bit of money from their customers—who willingly hand it over. Whole lot of these men gonna have lighter pockets by the end of the night, if not plain empty. They may not know it, but as soon as they walked in here, they never had a chance. The group I'm expecting has to be coming here. Got it on good information they would. Just need to bide my time. My doubts are still nagging me when they finally push through the door. I sit up, squinting to make sure. No doubt about it. That's them.

The first one in is a trim dark-skinned man with long hair like a Choctaw. But he's a Hindoo, I can tell, those other Indians from the Far East. More than a few of the women glance at his pretty face, and he flashes back a smile that makes even me blush. Didn't even know men could have eyelashes that long. At his side is a tall broad black man with a shadowy beard peppered over with white and a serious-set face. The old-time blue military jacket with gold epaulets marks him as a Haitian; his countrymen in the room raise their drinks in salute and he answers with a deep nod, his stone face unchanging. Behind the men are two more figures: one is the biggest Chinaman I ever put eyes on, wearing a tall wide-brimmed tan cowboy hat, of all things, and a long matching frock coat; the other—she turns out to be exactly who I came all this way to see.

The captain of the airship Midnight Robber is as tall as I remember—not so much as most men, but a good height. She wears snug-fitting tan britches on long lean legs, and the red and green jacket of a Free Isles flyer. Her coils of black hair are pulled back by metal clasps above a dark brown face with the kind of big eyes men like talking about. She scans around the place, one hand dropping to rest on a pistol at her waist. At a call from the Hindoo, she moves to join her group, walking with a slight limp. The other men in the room look her over, some curious, others admiring. Seems they uncertain if she's up for sale too. But she ignores them, instead shouting for a drink and settling into a sofa. Some of Shá Rouj's finest wares soon arrive, one of them squealing as she falls into the captain's lap. A stab of jealousy from Oya startles me. I push it away, trying to focus.

Now what? The information I got is something I'm certain this group will be keen on. And I have it in my mind to make a trade. But not like this. Too many eyes here. I glance to the Confederates. Seems they noticed the captain too. And they're doing a bad job at not staring. Definitely too many eyes. No, I'll have to wait to get her alone. I settle back, finishing my meal and trying to be patient.

I blink awake. Images of me in a burgundy dress dancing with a machete in the middle of a thunderstorm melt away with my dream. I'm thankful at least it's not about giant skulls in the sky. I curse beneath my breath, though, blaming Madame Diouf a little, and myself more, for dozing off. A hot bath and a full stomach? What was I thinking! Thankfully, I look around to find the crew of the *Midnight Robber* just where I'd left them. The Hindoo is standing on a table, drunk off his ass and reciting something like he's a theatre actor. The women around him clap while the Jack Tars roar in approval. But damn my luck, the captain's gone! I search the room. Could she have returned to her airship? No, not by herself. Remembering the woman in her lap, my gaze moves to an upper floor. Of course.

I push away from the table and walk through the kitchen to the back door. Heading outside, I make a half-circle around Shá Rouj 'til I find a good spot on the railing to pull myself up. My nickname on the streets is Creeper, and for good reason. Just like ma maman in the sweet gum tree, I'm a damn good climber. Got people to saying I remind them of one of those creeping vines that make their way up the side of buildings. Tonight, my nickname does me well. Didn't want to take the stairs right there in the open. No one's watching out here, though.

Reaching the second floor I hoist myself onto a balcony and peek inside a window. Some bodies moving in the shadows make Oya titter. Not the right ones, though. Takes about three more bits of peeping 'til I find my captain. She's lying facedown on a bed, her back rising slightly with her snores. Movement makes me pull away quick. A second woman is getting up from the bed. She walks to bend over a white porcelain basin on a dresser and spends some time washing before slipping her meager clothing back on. After deftly lacing up a frilly corset in a mirror, she stops to lay a kiss on the captain's bare shoulder before leaving.

Now's my chance. Pulling open the shutters I lift the window and ease myself into the dark room, taking care not to get my coat caught on anything. When my shoes touch the floorboards there's a creak that makes me wince, but I gingerly begin to make my way over. My mind races, trying to think of the best way to wake the sleeping woman I've gone through all this trouble to see. She solves my dilemma for me.

"Don't take another blasted step," a singsong Free Isles accent warns. The captain rises up from the bed and I find myself staring down the skinny barrel of a gold-plated pistol. I can't help admiring the gilded handiwork—Free Isles issue. She reaches up to turn a handle on the wall, pumping gas into a pair of hanging lamps. We both squint at the brilliance.

"What the ass?" she asks in surprise. "I thinking you is a bandit or a jumbie, but you just a boy?"

"Girl," I correct, tilting my head to let the light take in

my face: baby cheeks, small mouth, round lips and all.

"Girl, then," the captain repeats, unfazed. She doesn't even stop to button up her corset. Her large eyes look me up and down, passing judgment. And she hasn't put the gun away. "Somebody hire you to come here and steal from me nah? Put a knife in me neck?"

I shake my head. That odd bit of jealousy comes again from Oya. But there's a strange familiarity too. "Here to see you," I tell her. "I got information. Information to trade."

She frowns like she don't believe. "What you have to trade with me?"

I hesitate. I'd seen this discussion going different, certainly not under gunpoint. Figure now ain't the time to play coy. "The Black God's Drums," I blurt out.

That gets her interest, for sure. Slowly, the captain lowers her pistol, her face flat and unreadable. Refastening the buttons on her corset, she grabs a white shirt from the brass bedpost and begins slipping it on. "Talk," she orders. "Now." Her voice is alert, with a tone that says she's not having any nonsense. So, I talk.

"I like to sleep up on one of Les Grand Murs," I begin. "There are alcoves there no one checks, where I can see airships come in everyday. I like watching the people—"

"Good place for a thief to mark she victims," the captain cuts in wryly.

Well yes, I think, but that's beside the point. And rather rude to point out. "Saw you and your crew get off this morning," I continue. "Two nights back though, saw something else—a Confederate airship."

The captain shrugs. "New Orleans open to them jackass like everybody else."

"It's who's waiting for them," I explain. "A Cajun with white hair. He brings the Confederates down to my alcove. If I hadn't been tucked into my corner they'd have seen me. But they don't. And I listen to them talk. Confederates say they're here to get the Black God's Drums. Cajun says there's a Haitian scientist willing to exchange it for something."

The captain's brow furrows. "Exchange for what? Money?"

I shake my head. "Not money. They were talking about a jewel."

The captain goes quiet for a while. Her eyes are set on me but I can tell her mind is elsewhere. When she finally speaks, it's a question. "You know what that is—the Black God's Drums?"

I nod. I'd put it together plenty quick as soon as I heard it.

"Shango's Thunder," I answer. In my head, Oya dances at hearing her husband's name.

I used to ask ma maman to tell me the story over

and over again, about how Haiti had gotten free. She would talk about the mulatto inventor Duconge, who was raised up in France but returned to the island where his mother was born as a slave and offered his inventions to the black generals of the uprising. When Napoleon's armada came to take back the island they saw dozens of cannons on the highest hills, all shooting into the air. The Frenchies laughed, thinking the blacks couldn't aim. They stopped laughing though when the sky turned dark as night, and a storm came that wiped them from the sea. *Like the hand of an angry god,* ma maman would say.

"In Haiti, the weapon is named for other gods of storms—like Hevioso from Dahomey and Nsasi of Kongo," the captain relates. "But in Trinidad we name it for Shango, the Yoruba orisha of thunder. Name seem to catch on."

Oya grumbles with indignation across my thoughts: something about haughty Dahomey and upstart Kongo gods. Wasn't just them or Shango. She was there too, dancing in the whirlwind, dashing those Frenchie ships to bits and sending thousands of men to lay with Yemoja beneath the sea. Them Frenchies still down there with her mother now, she says, their bones and spirits held close.

"Only a few know its secret code name," the captain goes on. "'The Black God's Drums.'"

"Well, that scientist is going to give your secret weapon to some Rebs," I say.

Her face goes grim. "That's no good," she murmurs. "That's no good for nobody."

That last part I already know. Anything that helps those Rebs is bad trouble. I was born after the Armistice of Third Antietam, when the Union and Confederates, all battered up and starving from eight years of war, had called a truce. Might have been good for the white folk, but it doomed those blacks what hadn't made it to the Union. I've seen the tintype photographs from inside the Confederacy. Shadowy pictures of fields and factories filled with laboring dark bodies, their faces almost all covered up in big black gas masks, breathing in that drapeto vapor. It make it so the slaves don't want to fight no more, don't want to do much of nothing. Just work. Thinking about their faces, so blank and empty, makes me go cold inside.

"So what you want trade with me for this, lickle gal?" the captain asks.

I frown. Who's she calling lickle? No longer under the gun, I move to sit in a chair and lean back—trying to look casual and at ease. "I want to go with you when you leave," I say.

That makes her eyebrows rise. "Go with me? Go where?"

"On your airship, the *Midnight Robber.* I want to be crew."

She screws up her face, looking at me as if I've jumped out my skin and done a bloody jig around the room—then laughs. The sound makes me bristle. "What I want with a lickle gal on me ship?" She gives a brief, sharp suck of her teeth. "You think I want pickney to mind?"

"I don't need minding," I snap, my temper getting the better of me. Oya disagrees, whispering a lullaby. I push it away.

The captain leans forward, pinning me with her gaze. Those large eyes are as dark as Madame Diouf's. "You ever been on an airship?" she asks gruffly. "Know one end of it from the other?"

That wasn't fair. "I learn fast!" I counter.

The captain shakes her head, pursing her lips and this time sucking her teeth for a long while—the way old Creole women and Madame Diouf do. "What schupidness is this? Girl like you should be in school, learning your maths and letters, not gallivanting about on some airship! What your mother and father would say?"

"Nothing," I retort, biting each of my words so they're forced out. "They're dead." This sends her quiet. "Papa died in one of the tempêtes noires." *You took him, Oya,* I accuse. The goddess don't deny it. Just keeps humming.

"I never knew him. The yellow fever took ma maman three years back."

The captain searches my face for truth and decides she's found it. "I sorry for that," she says at last. "Still—"

"You knew her," I break in. I take off my cap and step further into the light. "Ma maman. She used to work here, for Madame Diouf. And the two of you ..." No need to say the rest.

The captain looks puzzled for a moment. But when she sees my face fully those already large eyes go even bigger.

"Rose," she whispers, speaking my mother's name. She stares, as if only now truly seeing me for the first time. "That same little nose and small eyes! Oh gosh, you Rose's daughter!" Then, more subdued, "I didn't know she had a child."

"Ma maman kept me away from her customers." This makes the captain flinch, but I just shrug. "It was work. She didn't have no shame in it. And I don't have no shame for her. I used to see you, though, coming here as crew with other Free Islanders, before you had your own airship. You couldn't have been much older than me."

"And how old is you now?" she probes.

"Sixteen," I declare, trying to sit up a little taller. She frowns dubiously. "Fine, fifteen," I amend. She frowns further. "Fourteen," I mutter. I refuse to admit thirteen.

The captain barks a laugh. "I was well past nineteen before I jumped on any airship! My grandmother would have put licks on my backside if I was even thinking it so young. At your age, all you should be studying on is your schooling and how some boy might like you so and dreaming about when you marry."

I make a face. Next thing she'll have me in frilly dresses and ribbons. "You don't seem to like boys," I remark.

This actually makes her smile. Her teeth are straight and white as pearls. "Don't think because you playing sneak-foot behind me that you does know my mind," she reprimands in a firm tone. "I like boys—men. Sometimes. And I get my schooling!"

"So, you plan to get married?" I say mockingly, folding my arms.

She snorts loudly. I almost smirk at that. Hard not to admire a woman who's not afraid to let out a good snort. "Not if I can help it. Eh! Stop with all these blasted questions! I a grown woman, and I don't need answer to you!" I watch as she swings her legs over the edge of the bed. And it's then I notice one of them isn't whole. Her right leg is only a thigh of smooth brown skin fitted snug into a metal casing; the rest is made of twisting copper rods that flex like muscle and bone. There's a steel ball joint where a knee should be and the calf is covered by a leather brown boot. So that explains the limp. She didn't have that when she visited before. I open my mouth to ask about it then clamp it back shut. None of my business.

She looks up to me, noticing my staring—and suddenly there's light. Gold like the sun, so much it hurts my eyes. She's bathed in it, all through her twisted coils of hair and covering her skin. I blink and the light's gone, leaving twinkling stars in her eyes. In my head Oya thunders, pushing words from my lips I don't mean to speak aloud.

"Bright Lady!" I blurt out before I can stop myself. The rest blares through my thoughts. *Oshun! The Bright Lady! Mistress of Rivers! Oya's sister-wife! Shango's favorite!* How hadn't I noticed it before? So that explained Oya's odd emotions, the jealousy and familiarity. More than one goddess shared this room.

The captain goes stiff as a beam at my words and her eyes narrow. So she knows about the goddess hovering about her, then. I can see it in her face, in the way her lips are pressed together all tight. But she hasn't accepted it. Well, that's none of my business either. I turn my head and say no more.

The magic of those old Afrikin gods is part of this city, ma maman used to say, buried in its bones and roots with the slaves that built it, making the ground and air and waterways sacred land. Only we forgot the names that went with that power we brought over here. Since Haiti got free, though, those gods were coming back, she'd said, across the waters, all the way from Lafrik. Now here's two of them in a bordello in New Orleans. Who knows what that means.

In the awkward quiet, the captain stands to slip back on her britches, then her remaining boot. "I'm going to find my crew," she tells me finally. "See if they think you talking true or just trying to sell me one big nancy-story. Wait here. I'll be back."

She buttons her Free Isles jacket and walks to the door.

"What's your name?" I call out quickly.

The captain turns back to me, hesitant before deciding. "Ann-Marie," she answers. "Ann-Marie St. Augustine."

"I'm Creeper," I reply. She pauses at that. Everyone does. But she nods.

I wait until she's gone. Then I disappear through the window into the night.

~

The next morning, I sit at the telegraph station near the Cabildo on Chartres Street in Emancipation Square. It's the most used one in the city, where all the finely dressed ambassadors and diplomats in top hats go to get their encrypted messages. If I figure things right, the captain should be here. I idle my time reading the day's *Crescent* broadsheet. Front page is mostly filled up with all the festivities, today being the Monday before the Maddi grá. Everybody just waiting for King Kwamena and King Deslondes to arrive on the Big Miss and lead the Night March, honoring the slave uprising of Afrikins and Creoles way back in 1811. The celebration used to kick up such a ruckus—what with all the poorer folk, street people, Guilde gangs, and like involved—that it got banned. But the City Council brung it back and made it proper, so that "respectable ladies and gentlemen"—so the broadsheet say—can take part. Say it's a good way to remember the unity that keep free New Orleans strong.

I'm dusting the sugar off my fingers from some beignets and folding away the papers when the captain shows up around midmorning, alone. She's easy enough to pick out, in that red and green Free Isles jacket ending at her waist with gold running on the lapels and cuffs. And there's that limp. After going inside the telegraph station, she returns some time later, head down and reading a letter.

"What does it say?" I ask, sidling up beside.

She whirls about to see me, then glowers, those big eyes scolding. "I tell you to wait last night!"

"So you could hand me over to Madame Diouf?" I accuse. "How stupid you think I am?"

She don't deny the charge, instead muttering, "Yuh a hard-headed child."

"And you don't answer questions," I retort, nodding to the telegraph. "What does it say?"

I'm half expecting her to drag me back to Shá Rouj. But instead she grunts and answers: "That your story right. There's a scientist in Haiti missing in truth. A man name Doctor Duval. He works on hydrometeorology and low altitude atmospheric modification. Might be the same one you hear about."

Hydro-Alti-Atmo what? The string of words make me dizzy just hearing them. But I keep my face blank—something you learn to do out here on the streets—as if I understand her plain as the day. "So what are we going to do?"

She looks back down, eyebrows raised. "We? We not doing anything. I done send out some of my crew to ask around about this white-haired Cajun man."

I make a scoffing sound, rolling my eyes for emphasis. "That Hindoo, the stone-faced Haitian, and the big Chinaman?"

"Nogai a Mongolian," the captain responds. Catching my quizzical look before I can hide it, she explains. "The one you calling a Chinaman. He not Chinese."

I try to shrug it off. "What's the difference?"

"A whole wall," she remarks dryly. "You see? This is

why you need your schooling."

I sigh. That again? "Fine, Mongolian. Anyway, no one's going to tell *them* anything. New Orleans folk don't talk to outside folk about our business. And those three stick out like a big old caiman at a rooster's ball." I pause, waiting to add the last words: "Besides, I already know where your scientist is."

The captain's head whips around to me, her eyes wider than I ever seen. She lunges at me then—grabbing my jacket and almost lifting me off my feet. Her swiftness catches me by surprise and Oya lashes out before I can stop her. There's a rush of wind and the captain is pushed away, stumbling back on her booted heels and dropping me. She seems dazed for a moment but then starts at me again, eyes blazing.

"I only just found out!" I say, backing off. Damn, the woman is quick! "I'll take you there now! Just tell me we have a deal on me joining your crew!" She's not stopping and a small bit of me starts to panic. "People are watching!" I hiss.

The captain stops then, just noticing the stares we're getting from passersby. Her face is a storm cloud. And for the first time, I'm all too aware she is a grown woman—quite taller than me and stronger too, much stronger. She seems to be thinking something over in the moment of silence that stretches on forever. Finally, clenching her fists and taking a deep breath, she says in a tight voice, "I'll think on it."

For a moment, all I can do is stare. She'll *think* on it? That's it? I go through all this trouble and she'll *think* on it? I want to shout back that she better *think* on it fast or there's no deal. But that fierceness in her face says I best not. I know well enough when to press and when not to. And that ain't no face ready to be pressed. I decide that *think* on it will have to do—for now.

"Let's go, then," I say grudgingly, heated at being grabbed and even more about giving in.

"Go where?" the captain demands, refusing to move. "How you know where he is?"

That could get a little messy if I have to explain. "I have a source," is all I reply.

Her face turns even more suspicious, if that was possible. "What kind of source?"

"The kind I can't tell you about." It's the same way I knew your airship would be arriving, I want to say, but keep that to myself.

"And how I know you not lying?"

I throw up my hands. Could this woman be any more stubborn? "What good would lying do me? If you don't find your scientist, I don't have anything to trade! I want to find him as much as you do!"

That seems to settle her doubts. I hope. At least for the

moment. She motions for me to lead the way, but her face never changes.

We walk down narrow streets bordered by a mix of buildings that carry pieces of New Orleans's history: colourful two-story Creole structures with gilded balconies, patterned Spanish arches, narrow flat-fronted redbrick American townhouses, even big stone monstrosities with ancient-looking columns and scowling gargoyles. It's all mostly quiet now, but come tonight and tomorrow these streets will be filled with people. Some are already masked, a few in headdresses of long feathers and others in the guises of animals, crescent moons, golden suns and other things. They dance in their ones and twos, wandering about to a set of goat-faced musicians blaring trumpets and strumming banjos. I hope we're done with this business in time for me to catch the festivities. Might be one of my last for a while. I glance up to the captain's face to find those storm clouds haven't cleared none.

"You still angry." I sigh. No response. "I didn't tell you about where the scientist was because I thought you'd leave me behind."

She waves me off. "I not mad about that—much."

I look over her face again, reading it properly this time. "You're mad at the scientist. That he would sell your secrets."

She glares at me for a bit, like she's angry all over again that I figured it out. Then she nods in admission. "That he ah traitor, yes. But more than that. What he doing, it damn irresponsible. Shango's Thunder not something to play with."

"If it's so powerful," I venture, "then why don't Haiti just give it to the Union? That way they could just whip those rebels and end the war for good. Everyone knows Haiti and the Free Isles run weapons up North. That you help supply old General Tubman in her guerilla war, blowing up Confederate munitions and smuggling out slaves. No matter what the armistice say. Figure that's what you do on your airship."

Her eyes narrow. "Oh yes? What make you think so? More sneak-foot business?"

"Don't take no sneaking." I point to the pistol in her holster. "That gun's Free Isles issue, made for privateers. Your ship's a cargo freighter, but I didn't see you unload anything. Bet you aren't taking on much either. That's kind of funny, ain't it? And no ordinary airship captain gets encrypted wires from Port-au-Prince."

A slight smirk plays on her lips. She's impressed. Annoyingly, I find myself pleased at this and try not to smile back. "After France lose she fleet, she was set on getting back she colony," the captain relates as we walk. "Napoleon send out three times as many ships as before, and he get all the great powers to join him. They was enemies, yes. But they come together to destroy Haiti. America agree too, even if she don't take part. When Dessalines hear about that big fleet coming he know he can't stop it with he small navy. All he generals say, let loose the Black God's Drums! Turn the sky black again!" She stops to shake her head. "But Dessalines 'fraid that power. He 'fraid it too bad. When it use the first time, the storm not only mash up France's fleet, it come up on land, cut through the whole island, kill hundreds—men, women, children. Storm don't care who it take, you hear? It swallow up everything in it way."

"That's how General Toussaint died," I put in.

The captain nods gravely. "The old people in Haiti say when the Black God's Drums loose again, Papa Toussaint going to rise from the sea and lead an army of jumbie to conquer the whole world!" The thought sets Oya to rumbling laughter, and flashes of ghosts on horseback, galloping up from the waves to sweep across whole cities, fill my head. "So instead, Dessalines have he inventor, Duconge, make him another weapon—great big air balloons cast out of iron, filled with the very same gas we airships does use now. And each balloon carry men with the green sticky-sticky fire. Those balloons sail out one morning from Haiti and drop that sticky-sticky fire down on the invading armada right on the water." She makes a whooshing sound, snapping her fingers. "It light all them ships up like a match—burn up everything. Men jump into the sea to get away, but the sticky-sticky fire keep burning even in the water. None of them leave alive! When Dessalines threaten to send those iron balloons across the sea and set fire to London and Paris, real fear catch the whites for the first time. They beg for peace. Dessalines demand they pay a big ransom, too—millions of francs. He make them give up all their slave colonies in the Caribbean, and the Free Isles was born."

I know that part. Everyone do. Lots of folk still name their sons—daughters too—for Dessalines. "So no one's ever used Shango's Thunder again?" I ask. "Not since that one time?"

"No one schupid enough to do that," the captain responds darkly. "These black storms that come every year now, what allyuh does call tempêtes noires. The ones that make your city build these big walls to protect itself. That some of Shango's Thunder still in the skies. Houngan-scientists in Haiti say loosing that power just that one time mess up the whole weather. Just that one time, you see! If we start using it to fight . . ." She trails off, shaking her head.

She don't need to finish. I ain't like the more well-off that can leave New Orleans when the tempêtes noires come, so I been through them every year. Spent enough time in the city shelters, clutching onto people I don't even know and listening to them pray as the winds beat on the walls around us—sounding like a steam train about to plow right through. When I hold on to them, it's not because I'm afraid. It's because of Oya. She likes them black storms. And when they come, it's all I can do to control myself. Truth is, I want to run out in the streets and dance in all that wind and rain, even knowing it'll dash me to pieces. So, I stay in the shelter with people, so I can keep hold of myself.

"Why you so set on coming on my ship?" the captain asks. The shift in topic catches me off guard. "This is where you raise up," she goes on. "Why you want to leave it?"

Fair enough question, I admit. I never been out of New Orleans, not once. Most other people I know can't imagine being nowhere else. Talk about the city like nothing else exists. But spending time up on Les Grand Murs, watching all the airships and people coming in, make me want to see as much of this big world as I can. That don't mean I like New Orleans any less, though. It's too much to say, I decide. And I'm not sure how. I answer instead with my own question: "What made you leave your home?"

The captain shrugs. "Trinidad nice. Real nice. But it not big enough to hold me. Whole world is my island."

"Same for me," I say. She looks down and for once there's

something in those dark eyes like understanding. Then something else is in there, something more guarded. It takes her a while to speak, and when she do her voice is low.

"Last night, you say something to me about Oshun," she all but whispers.

There it is. I figured that had to come up sometime. Oya and her mouth!

I just nod. If she want me to say more, she'll have to do the asking.

"How do you know? Is she . . . with you too?"

I shake my head. "For me, Oya."

The captain's eyes rise but settle just as quick. She don't look like the type that stays surprised too long. "The sister," she mutters. "That explain some things." Her face folds into a frown, inspecting me up and down. "You some kind of santera or mambo? So young they does make you here?"

"I'm not any of those things. The goddess is just . . . with me."

"Like you possessed?"

It's my turn to frown up at the woman. "You know that's not how it works."

She huffs, muttering: "Yes, yes. Have to let them in. Don't understand how all of them can be with we, and with they priests and all over the blasted place at the same time."

"They're gods," is all I answer. Really, it's not complicated. I figured a long time back that what's inside me isn't the whole goddess Oya. Don't think nobody could have all of her inside them. And she's not just in one place either. She's too vast and too big for that. I think it's more like parts of her can be in many places at once, each of them different—but also the same, so that one set of people might even call her other names or see her with a different face. But even so, she's always Oya. Alright, so maybe it is complicated.

"It don't bother you, then?" the captain presses. "Having she inside you? Knowing what you thinking?"

Bother? I turn the strange question over in my head. Like asking if I'm bothered by my right arm. Me and Oya might quarrel some, but I can't imagine putting up the fight this captain do. No wonder she's always frowning.

"It's not always easy," I admit. The one thing Oya definitely isn't is easy. "The goddess can be fickle. Most times she got her own mind, pulling me one way while I'm trying to go another. We don't always see eye to eye. But not having her with me would be . . ." I search for the right words. "I would feel alone."

If the captain has anything else to say I don't get to hear it, because we arrive just then.

"We're here," I inform her, stopping at the mouth of a backstreet that opens out onto a main road. Across from us is the railway station for the New Orleans and Carrollton train lines. There's long double-deck carriage cars too, some with small steam engines and others pulled by horses. Both will take you all around the city and to nearby towns. Boardinghouses for travelers line the block. I point to a small white one with a bright yellow sign that reads Chez Voyajer. That's where my source tells me a Haitian man has been staying for the past two days, sometimes visited by a white-haired Cajun. I tell the captain as much.

"This source of yours tell you what he look like?" she questions.

Before I can answer a small black man steps out of the side door of the boardinghouse. He's dressed in a long dark coat over a blue suit, topped with a hat like a stovepipe. He holds a large red carpetbag to him while looking around as if waiting for someone. The captain and I exchange a knowing glance—and then she starts out for him.

I hiss for her to wait. There's people everywhere! But she's already gone. Cursing, I dash forward and almost get run over by a bulky covered wagon. I jump back from the trotting horses just in time, glowering up at the driver—and then stop dead as recognition hits. It's the tall man in the black mortician's suit! The same one from last night! He's still wearing that skeleton mask and I can hear him humming that odd song. When his blue eyes turn to glance down at me, memories of Oya's strange vision fill my head. And I see that grinning skull—now his face, those ice blue eyes where empty black sockets once was—rising above New Orleans like a great big moon, swallowing up everything in its shadow. Something about his stare pins me where I stand, like something done took hold of me and drove stakes through my feet into the ground. And all I can do is stare back, unable to move. If he remembers me at all, I can't tell, because he just turns away and finishes up parking the wagon.

It's not until his eyes are off me that I can move again. Stumbling as my feet start working, I angle around and run to catch up to the captain. I reach her just as she gets to the small black man, grabbing him by the arm and spinning him about. He jumps at her touch, eyeing her from behind round iron-rimmed spectacles.

"Doctor Duval?" The words are more an accusation than a question.

"Wi?" the man stammers. His Haitian accent is unmistakable. "You work for them?"

"Oh, I work for somebody," the captain snaps. "You seem lost. And I here to get you back to Port-au-Prince, Doctor Duval."

At this the small man rears back, throwing up his

hands. "No! I cannot! Not yet! I haven't gotten my jewel!"

"I don't care about your blasted jewel!" the captain growls. "We going, and now!"

She has a firm grip on the small man's arm. And I'm pretty certain that if it comes to a fight, she'll best him easy. But he isn't looking at her anymore. Something else has caught his attention. I turn to follow his gaze down the street, opposite from where the wagon's parked. There are men coming. About half a dozen. The one in front is a sun-tanned white man in plain clothes and a woven straw hat, with white hair beneath. The Cajun. The others trailing him I recognize all too well. Confederates. Yup, the same ones from Shá Rouj, even if they no longer wearing their uniforms. Pretty sure they one and the same with the men in my alcove too. I add it up in my head and find I don't care for the bill. Them, the man in the skeleton mask, and Oya's vision. All coming together in this same place, at the same time. And us here standing right between them. Something's not right. I can feel it: a tingling in the air like the kind that come right before a storm. I open my mouth to shout a warning, to tell the captain we need to go, quick. And suddenly Oya is there, filling up my thoughts.

The world slows and time takes to crawling on her belly.

The men walking towards me look like corpses now, with pale dead faces. Their steps are twisted and shuffling. And they're no longer on the street. Instead, they're all heading towards a cemetery of tall crypts that litter the ground like bones, the once white stone stained and weathered by rain as distant music plays. Oya dances in front of them, her feet moving to a pounding rhythm of drums, her legs taking deep strides and her arms swirling this way and that. She's wearing a long crimson dress that's being whipped about by a furious wind as she leads the silent men with haunted eyes on the way to their resting place. Just as quick as it came, the vision disappears. Oya's gone. So is the cemetery. And the dead men are alive again, walking towards us on the street. I turn around just in time to see the man in the skeleton mask pull the canvas off the covered wagon, revealing three hidden figures inside. They're wearing skeleton masks too, and standing behind the biggest gun I ever seen. It's pointed right in our direction. I don't bother shouting anymore, I just shove the captain hard with my shoulder and knock her down to the road.

Then the bullets come.

The morning quiet is broken with the deafening bap-bap-bap! of the Gatling. It don't hit us though. The bullets instead sail clear over our heads, hissing as they go, and catch their real targets. I watch the Cajun go down first, his white hair smeared in spatters of his own blood. The Confederates behind him get much the same. Their bodies remind me of dancing marionettes I once seen. The bullets make them jerk while standing up before dropping like their strings been cut. I seen enough. I practically drag the captain with me, and we scramble off the road to take cover behind a carriage. The frightened horse attached to the thing is screaming and kicking, its eyes rolling in terror as it tries to break free. People out on the streets are screaming too, running every which way. The shooting's stopped and I watch two of the skeleton-masked men jump from the wagon. They make for the Haitian scientist—I didn't even realize we'd lost him. He never moved, just laid flat there on the road, shaking all over with his hands covering his head. Grabbing his arms, the men in the skeleton masks hoist him up and run back to the wagon with his feet dragging between them. When they reach it they dump him inside like a sack before climbing in to join him.

Beside me the captain has her pistol out. She's shimmering with Oshun's light, all gold and bright. And her eyes are wilder than the horse's. She has the look of someone ready to run into battle no matter the odds and whatever may come. Her blood is up, and though she may not know it, the goddess she carries is stirred up too. I know how she's feeling with all that power inside: like you riding a bolt of lightning, like you tied to something bigger than you can even describe, like you can go up against anything. Only feeling some way don't make it so. She starts to rise and I grab her gun hand, jerking it down and pointing with emphasis to the Gatling that's trailing smoke. She relents, seeming to grudgingly accept that if that thing is turned on us her pistol won't help. The light around her vanishes and she crouches back down out of sight. Together, we watch the wagon speed away, driven by the grinning skeleton man. He's whipping his horses so hard that they gallop and almost trample anyone in their way. All the while, I can hear him singing at the top of his lungs:

> *"And when the people hear the gun!*
> *The men and boys they all will run!*
> *Expecting for to see the fun!*
> *When they get there will all as one!*
> *Huzza! for Andrew Jackson!"*

When he disappears down the street, I release a breath I think I been holding since the shooting began. My chest hurts and my heart feels like it's going to pound right out my insides and flop about. I look out at the bodies of the dead Confederates and the Cajun lying bloody in the street, remembering the ghostly images. Oya rules over the cemetery as much as she does the winds. The meaning of *this* vision don't take much to figure out.

Next time, I tell her, you could be quicker with the warning! My mind, however, is already spinning with what all this could mean. That man in the skeleton mask—I know now he's the one from Oya's vision the other night. But what he and those other men got to do with any of this? And why would they kill a bunch of Confederates? They'd taken the scientist, so chances are they know who he is. This don't make sense. It's just one big tangled jumble sitting there in my head. And I need answers. I turn to go but the captain grabs me, bringing me up short.

"Eh! Where you think you going?" she barks, holding fast to my coat. I call up Oya's winds. But they don't come like before. There's still a lingering jealousy from the goddess, but it's dull and faded. Now there's a feeling towards the captain that's almost . . . sisterly. I groan. Should have known whatever disagreements or troubles these two got, it wouldn't last long.

"What just happen here?" the woman demands angrily. "Who the hell was that?"

"I don't know!" I answer truthfully. My first thought is one of the Guildes. But I didn't recognize their skeleton dress. And Guildes don't have guns—not like that, nohow. "I need to go—talk to my source!"

"Oh yes!" the captain agrees. "But I going with you, you hear? No more of this damn sneak-about business!"

I glare up at her but she only glares back. Frustratingly, Oya seems to find this all agreeable. No help there. I glance around to see constables running from up the street and hear the telltale clanging of an approaching mudbug. Can't stay here long. "Fine, then!" I give in. "But we have to go—now!"

We leave the railway, heading back into the Quarter. I move quick, hoping I might lose the captain in the maze of backstreets. Besides, thinking of that man in the skeleton mask makes me not want to see anyone in a costume right now. But she keeps up easy, even with her mechanical leg. Still, it's a long go. And we're both short of breath by the time we arrive.

"What's this place?" she asks when we come to a stop. She's staring up at the large two-story Creole town house of wood and stone in front of us. It's painted white, with a pitched roof and a balcony ringed by a banister on its upper floor. On the very top of the building is a big cross made of iron. The dark metal catches bits of sunlight that reflect off it like a shiny crown.

"A convent," I answer. "The Sisters of the Sacred Family."

She twists her head to frown down at me. "Your source is a nun?"

"Two nuns," I correct. "They watch the city. I mean, they watch *over* the city."

The captain's jaw goes slack for a moment, open like she's trying to take in air.

"Nuns," she repeats, disbelieving. "Who watch over the city?"

"Yes," I reply. "Oh, and there's Féral. Be careful with her. She bites."

She glares as if I've not made a bit of sense, but follows me into the building.

~

A short time later we're seated at a table in the lower kitchens of the convent. It was probably a nice table once, with flowery carvings all over like ma maman used to like. But now the gold paint is peeling, and I pick at the bits absently to see the yellowing wood underneath. Spices mixed with the hickory scent of wood burning in black stoves hang in the air of the hot room. And my stomach rumbles when I look to the boiling cast-iron pot on the fire, reminding me I haven't eaten nothing all day but some beignets. I pull my eyes away before my belly starts bawling even louder, and return them to plump Sister Agnès, who it seems has been talking now forever in her honey-sweet voice.

". . . and we became the only order of free women of colour in the parish—before such a thing was even legal," she's saying. "It was mostly quadroons and such back then. Our founder Sister Henriette was an octoroon herself. Her mother took her to fancy balls in this very place, when it was a ballroom. White men would fight duels up on the promenade over those coloured women! Scandalous!" Both chins on her round beige face tremble as she shakes her head beneath a black veil that drapes her like a hood. "Today we've turned this from a den of concubinage to a place of refuge. And we welcome all women, no matter caste or colour." She pauses, her blind eyes squinting as she touches a hand absently to a silver cross at her chest. "Sister Eunice, you've cut that okra much too small. Just a half-slice will do, non?"

A thin woman, in a long black tunic like Sister Agnès, complete with that white covering over her neck and shoulders, looks up from where she's chopping and tossing things into a skillet. "Lese mwen trankil!" she snaps. "I've cut them fine! Been making gumbo a long time. Longer than you!"

"That doesn't mean you always get it right," Sister Agnès reprimands her gently.

Sister Eunice's brown face tightens up and her lips pucker. "You can't even *see* me cutting it."

"That's rude," Sister Agnès says. "For Lent this year, I

suggest you give up that sharp tongue, wi? Besides, I can *hear* you cutting."

Sister Eunice throws up her hands, dumping the okra with determination into the skillet. I just sit listening. I'm more than used to it. The two women are old enough to be my grandmaman. But they get on like this all the time.

"Féral, non!" Sister Agnès commands sternly. "You keep your fingers out of that pot!"

A scrawny young girl, wearing a ragged dress the color of faded moss, flinches. She pulls her hand away from the boiling gumbo and sits back on the floor with her skinny legs out in front. Her freckled face turns sulky and her two green eyes shrink to slits that stare out from behind a mess of long tangled hair, gold as straw. I make a face at the swamp girl, who's just a few years younger than me. She wrinkles her pug nose and sticks a pink tongue back out in turn.

"Mondjé!" Sister Agnès frets wearily. "Now where was I? Oh yes, so our order—"

"Sister," the captain cuts in. There's not much patience in her voice. I'm surprised she's lasted this long. "I don't mean to be rude, but I come here on important business."

"Important business," Sister Agnès repeats. She props her chins up on a set of plump fingers. "And what happens when that business has shoot-outs disturbing the morning's peace? Leaving men dead in our streets? Whose business is it then, Ann-Marie?"

The captain throws a startled glance my way and I shrug. The two odd sisters know everything that goes on in this city. Most of it comes from their charity work. Feed folk and they like to talk, I guess. They have more connections than anyone can count. It was them I came to when I overheard the talk between the Cajun and the Confederates, knowing they'd find out quick what was going on. They told me about the captain and her arriving airship, and where best to meet up with her. But how this morning's happenings reached the two before we even arrived, I can't begin to figure out.

"Enough of your prattle!" Eunice growls. She stomps over to stand in front of us, waving a dripping spoon. Féral leans forward, stretching to try and catch drops on her tongue. "This scientist you looking for, the Jeannots have him! They killed those Confederates and snatched him up right in front of you! Now he's somewhere in La Ville Morte and who knows what they have him doing! Nothing good! Mo sèrtin!"

Sister Agnès lets out another weary sigh. "You see? This is why I do the talking, Eunice. You just confused them."

The thinner sister rounds about, waggling her spoon. "Better than all your preening!"

"Jeannots?" the captain interrupts before they can

start up. "What's a Jeannot?"

That I already know. Knew it the minute Sister Eunice said the word. And I also know that means trouble. "Johnny Boys," I say, gritting my teeth. Those men in skeleton masks were Johnny Boys. And that means the tall man in the mortician's suit, the one from Oya's vision: he's a Johnny Boy too. *Damn it. Damn it. Damn it.*

"Johnny Boys?" the captain repeats, confused. "One of allyuh Guilde gang?"

I shake my head. It's worse than that.

"The Jeannots were originally a Confederate regiment," Sister Agnès answers, clearing her throat and taking back control. She seems happy to have something else to recite. "When the Confederacy signed the neutrality treaty with the Union and withdrew from New Orleans, not all of their soldiers agreed, especially those from the region. Some deserted to the swamps to carry on 'the cause.' Most of those original soldiers have died or drifted away now, of course. But there are those in the city who still haven't taken to the changes we've made. They slip off to the swamps and name themselves after the old regiment."

A bunch of fools who liked to play dress up and at soldiering, if you ask me. Most folk stayed clear of the swamp because of them, hollering and carrying on like banshees like they do. The city sent constables in to clear them out more than a few times, but never could get them all. "But how did the Jeannots even learn about the scientist?" I ask.

"I would look to your Cajun," Sister Agnès replies.

"Likely he was selling information to both sides," Sister Eunice adds. "To get an increase in his share."

"It get him dead," the captain snaps. "What these Jeannots want? Why they kill they own Confederates?"

"The Jeannots don't claim the Confederacy," Sister Agnès says. "They believe the Confederate States betrayed them by signing the treaty. They consider themselves patriots to Old New Orleans and hope to set up their own country right here. They used to carry out raids in the early days, riding around dressed as ghosts or skeletons to harass the former slaves. It caused quite a bit of trouble. People were beaten, even killed. The Jeannots took a blood oath: to take back the city or destroy it." She waves a hand in the air, twirling her fingers as if clearing away nonsense. "But the worst of that stopped years ago. We'd come to believe they'd abandoned most of their politics, and were now given to simply stealing and smuggling. Events this morning may have proven us . . . premature in our assessment. It may be that the taking of your scientist is a means for them to fulfill their oath."

I go back over the sister's words. The Jeannots took an oath: *to take back the city or destroy it.* Oya's vision replays before my eyes: a giant skeleton's grinning skull, rising to put out the lights of New Orleans. The pieces rattling around in my head suddenly fit together, and their meaning hits me all at once. "They want Shango's Thunder!" I exclaim in alarm, jolting up straight in my chair. "They're going to use it on the city!"

Sister Agnès nods gravely, confirming my fears. "So we believe. And yes Ann-Marie, Jacqueline told us about the weapon." I glance over to find the captain glowering at me and I shrug again. What'd she expect? You had to give information to get any from these two. "Fortunately for us," the sister goes on, "we have the both of you."

That catches our attention, and we whip our heads about as one to look at the nun.

She dips her head to me. "Touched by Our Lady Oya." Her head swivels to the captain. "Blessed by Our Lady Oshun. Think it's just by chance that you are both caught up in all this?"

At the stove Sister Eunice cackles. "Non! Non! Not just chance! Not just chance at all!"

The captain looks between the two women, her eyes narrowing. "Allyuh sure allyuh is nuns and not obeah women?" she asks.

Sister Agnès only smiles: a plump knowing angel. I say nothing. Like I said before about these sisters: they're odd.

"Gumbo ready!" Sister Eunice declares. "Lucky for you, Jacqueline and Ann-Marie, I always start a small pot early—before making the other sisters' midi meals. Just have to cut it five ways today." She spoons steaming gumbo into several small bowls and walks over to set them in front of us. My mouth waters at the smell.

"Mèsi! Mèsi!" Sister Agnès claps, receiving her bowl. "Now, Ann-Marie, let's discuss how you are going to retrieve this scientist and spirit him back home."

That takes me by surprise. "Shouldn't we warn the constables?" I ask. I don't hold much affection for lawmen, but this seems something they should handle.

Sister Agnès shakes her head. "Non. We can't have the authorities involved. Should the constables take up this matter, the City Council will have to oversee it. And the Council is filled with too many ambitious men. Some of them might take it into their fool heads to keep this scientist *and* his weapon. Oh, they'll say it's for the good of the city, mo sèrtin. But doing so will make New Orleans a threat to the Confederacy, to the Union, even perhaps Haiti and the Free Isles."

"Not to mention the other powers who might rethink the treaty that protects us," Sister Eunice puts in.

Sister Agnès shakes her head a second time. "We don't need any of that trouble here. The less who know of this weapon the better." She turns her head sharply. "Don't you agree, Ann-Marie?"

The captain returns a deep considering nod. I think Sister Agnès has finally impressed her. "The Free Isles and Haiti prefer this remain an internal matter," she affirms. "Besides, we not trying to have no big big fight. A small posse better for this. I can take some of me crew. Enough of we to handle these Jeannots."

"Tre byen!" Sister Agnès proclaims. "And Jacqueline will accompany you."

That's the second thing that takes me by surprise. The captain turns wary eyes my way. "I don't need the girl," she says. For once I don't argue. My part in our bargain is done. And I could do without a trip to the Dead City or getting caught up with Jeannots.

"Oh, you do," Sister Eunice disagrees, sitting down with her bowl. She jabs a silver spoon in our direction. "You both need each other. You just don't know it yet. Heh!"

I frown at her meaning, and want to protest. But in my head, I can hear Oya sliding her machetes one against the other. The sound of metal scraping on metal, slow but eager—readying for battle. I release a long inner sigh. Oya didn't send her visions lightly. Whatever that grinning skull moon meant, it involves these Jeannots. Should have seen that earlier. But I was too caught up in my own affairs to take notice of how it was all connected.

That means the sisters are right. I need to be there, like it or not.

"Not to worry," Sister Agnès says, cutting off the captain's ready objections. "We'll be sending you with some help. Sister Eunice? Do you have the items we managed to secure?"

The other nun's eyes widen and she sets down her gumbo, jumping up and running over to an old cast-iron pot-bellied stove in the corner of the room. It's all covered in rust, and don't look like it's used for cooking anymore. She stoops down to swing open its small iron door and reaches inside to pull out what looks like a baking pan covered in a bundle of black cloth. It takes two hands to lift it, and when she brings it back she puts it down gently on the table and takes off the covering.

Underneath, there are four long dark cylinders fitted into a tanned leather case. They remind me of the tall tin cans the factories use to put jellies and fruit in. Next to the case is a big clear glass flask with a long neck corked by black rubber and a wide round bottom, like the ones I seen at the apothecary shops. It's filled up less than halfway with some green liquid. Not just a regular green either, but a colour so bright it glows like a lamp. I'm not sure what I'm looking at exactly, and lean in to inspect it closer. The captain does the same—then suddenly rears back, coming to her feet and knocking over her chair in the process. She's staring at the green in that flask like it's a coiled-up swamp moccasin.

"Drapeto gas!" she hisses between clenched teeth.

I snap my neck back around to the glass flask in shock, and almost jump back myself—except I got a bowl of gumbo in my lap and don't intend to spill that. Drapeto! The stuff they use in the Confederate States on the slaves. To keep them from running away or rising up. To make them not want to do anything but work and do as they told. That's what's sitting on this table now, just a short ways from me. It makes my stomach knot up. And in my head, I hear Oya letting out a long string of Afrikin curses.

"Drapeto gas!" the captain exclaims again, like she's trying to make sense of it. She cuts narrow eyes to the nuns. "Allyuh know how dangerous this is?"

"Quite," Sister Agnès responds mildly. "That's why we keep it in a flask, Ann-Marie."

The captain shakes her head. "Haiti and the Free Isles trying for years now to get they hand on this. To get spies to smuggle it for we, so to study it. Maybe find a way to make it weak or deaden it. And the two of you have some keep up here in a kitchen in a convent?" Only thing that match the disbelief in her voice is the awe on her face.

"We have our contacts in the slave states," Sister Agnès replies, her voice even and calm as unbothered water.

I bet she do, I think. Everyone knows the sisters help smuggle in runaways from the Confederacy. "Though, this came to us by surprise. Not gas, as you can well see, but a liquid distillation, which likely becomes the gas." She stops, putting fingers to her temples. "But why am I talking? Sister Eunice can explain better than I. She has a head for this type of tinkering."

The other nun don't need no further urging to jump in. "Likely drapeto is made *as* a liquid," she says, pointing to the flask. "It's fitted into the masks—probably in canisters by what we've seen from designs—and then, by means of an additive, slowly made into vapor and passed through filters built into the mask to be inhaled."

My body lets loose a shudder that I can't help, my mind thinking again to the photographs I seen. Coloured men and women, even children, with those big black masks fitted on the bottom half of their face—with a long, rounded end that stick out in the front. All you can really see are their eyes. Eyes that look so blank and empty, like the real them is somewhere sunken deep inside, drowning in all that green gas. And they can't get out.

"I hear just the smallest bit of it take your mind away," I recite, remembering what I've heard. "Make it so that you walking but dead inside."

"Oh, it's not that potent," Sister Eunice assures me. "At

least not this batch we have here. From the tests we've done—" She stops, reading the wide-eyed looks both me and the captain are giving, then shakes her head. "Non! Non! Sister Agnès and I only tested it on each other!" That don't make our eyes go any smaller, but she continues. "From what we can tell, the liquid takes a good dose to have any real effect. And it leaves you in a matter of hours. But during that time, your mind is very susceptible to suggestions."

"It is an unpleasant sensation," Sister Agnès adds with a grimace.

"Wi," Sister Eunice agrees, though she sounds more curious than appalled. "But we think if adequately delivered, it could be used to proper advantage. To, say, take away the will to fight from an enemy?" Her fingers tap one of the dark canisters in the leather case, and for the first time, I realize those things ain't filled with jellies. They're filled with drapeto! The captain frowns but takes a few steps forward and reaches out a hand to gingerly run across the canisters.

"Would have to get up close to deliver it," she murmurs. "Maybe with a long rifle or—"

"Already solved," Sister Eunice proclaims. She takes out a canister and taps at a little silver handle fitted on top. "You pull at this and throw. Then boof!" She stops to make a sweeping gesture with her arms that makes me and the captain both jump. "Drapeto gas everywhere! Just be sure to have a mask on. My own invention."

She says the last part with a smug smile and the captain takes to staring at the two sisters, that disbelieving look on her face again. "The two of you is nuns?"

Sister Eunice lets out another cackle.

"Nuns with a few useful resources at our disposal," Sister Agnès puts in, a smirk tugging at the corner of her lips. "And we make good use of them as we can. We've also been supplied with a fairly good idea of where the Jeannots now reside. And we'll be sending Féral along as your guide." The captain and I share a glance. "Whatever faces the two of you are making, you can put an end to it," the nun scolds. "You'll have to travel La Ville Morte on foot I'm afraid. Your airship will just scare off the Jeannots and you won't be able to see a thing through that swamp, besides. Féral knows the Dead City probably better than anyone in this room. So she's going with you, and that's that."

We all turn to the girl who's sitting on the ground, slurping her gumbo messily and gnawing loud as ever on a crab leg.

"Féral!" Sister Agnès chides her. "Bon manyè! You know we wait for grace!" The girl scowls, wiping gumbo juice off her chin and lowering her bowl—but not the crab leg.

"What wrong with she?" the captain whispers. "She gone in the head or what?"

Sister Agnès blinks. "Wrong? Why nothing. Féral's just not very refined. She hadn't lived among people when we found her—wandering the swamp, you see. The convent wanted to put her out, after several, ah, incidents, with the other girls. But Sister Eunice and I convinced them to let us care for her. The Sisters of the Sacred Family welcome all, no matter caste or colour, or, for that matter, tameness. Despite her rough ways, she's a sweet child, in truth." She pauses. "But be careful. She bites."

The captain grimaces. "So I does hear."

Féral looks up, baring her teeth in a sharp smile, the end of a crab leg jutting out between them.

~

It's sundown by the time we start out into La Ville Morte, behind the big iron wall that borders Swamp Pontchartrain. The boatmen who bring us run contraband and runaway slaves on rafts and small canoes regular along the waterway. Mentioning the two nuns' names is enough to gain passage for cheap. They don't ask why we out here. Seem like they familiar enough doing work for the sisters. And probably figure the less they know the better.

Our first glimpse of the Dead City is stone buildings and houses rising up from black water far as you can see, covered in cypress trees and swamp moss. All this was supposed to be a new set of quarters stretching as far as Lake Pontchartrain. That was, until the first tempête noire come. No one expected that lake to rise up like it did, washing away everything and everybody in front of it. When the wall was raised up, they left that drowned city behind, abandoned with its dead. The swamp moved in right after to swallow up the rest—like it was just waiting for the people to leave to take back what belonged to it.

None of the boatmen are willing to go too far inside, not with night creeping up. Lots of folk see La Ville Morte as one big cemetery of the drowned—sacred ground with spirits who shouldn't be disturbed. We get dropped off just a ways in and the boatmen turn back, leaving us with wishes of luck and God's protection. We accept both and begin our walk through the Dead City.

It's me, the captain, the bearded Haitian, who I find out is named François, and the big Chinaman I now know is Mongolian, Nogai (cowboy hat and all), wading through what used to be the streets of La Ville Morte. Féral is our guide. She walks, sometimes even swims, through the swamp water, hardly making a sound or a splash. Every now and again she stops and gazes about, looking up at buildings of weather-stained stone with plants and whole trees growing out their open windows. She makes us stop too, with sharp grunts and hand gestures. That's about the most talking she ever do. Could be she's trying to find her way, or to keep us from the deep parts out here, where the ground drops away and we could well drown. We wait it out. Then, when she's good and satisfied, she starts up again and waves us to follow.

"She know where she going?" the captain asks, striding beside me through water that comes up to her hips. The Haitian and Mongolian follow behind, carrying long rifles and big bundled sacks strapped to their backs.

"Nobody knows the swamp or La Ville Morte better than the Hideaways," I point out, pushing through water that reaches to my middle. Thankfully the sisters were able to get me and Féral some sturdy boots to step through all this muck. Some good britches too, and dark blue jackets they say was for Union drummer boys back during the war. They fit a bit tight but still nice, and make it so I don't catch too bad of a chill. Kept my cap though. Don't go nowhere without that. Night's coming on quick now and it's getting so I can't barely make out much. But the swamp girl finds her way easy, taking us around moldering buildings and under whole trees that's slipped off their roots and lying longwise.

"Hideaways?" the captain asks.

"The white folk who ran off into the swamp," I explain. "People say when the uprising started against the Confederates, back during the war, all the big whites sent their families into La Ville Morte to hide with the house slaves. Only, those slaves run off to join the uprising and left them out here alone. Some of them white folk get so scared, they wandered deeper in and get lost—claim they heard rumors coloured people was killing all the whites or making slaves of them. They stayed and had children out here. And those children had children. Grow up wild as the swamp." I tilt my chin to indicate Féral. "Every now and again, some of them wander out."

The captain eyes me funny at hearing the tale. I just shrug. "Least, that's what people say—believe it or no."

She turns back to eye our guide, suspicion creeping over her face. "So is a granddaughter of a plantation owner leading we? Her mother was probably some mistress in a big house with a hundred slaves. Allyuh does trust she?"

Imagining the swamp girl dressed up all fancy like some plantation belle I seen in pictures almost makes me laugh. "Féral don't know nothing about any of that," I assure her. "She not no plantation mistress. She just Féral, is all."

The captain seems to accept that, though she glances

every now and then at the small girl as if expecting her to vanish and leave us lost. Most times, though, she's got her eyes on the waters or turning her head real quick like she hear something. She seem bothered and uneasy. At least more than usual. The swamp will spook you like that, if you let it.

We make our way around what used to be a church. All that's left are walls, with clumps of hanging moss and vines growing through them like long twisting worms. You can see where some swamp birds made nests in its windows, and they look down at us like we trespassing on their home. There's a stretch of quiet, and I listen as the swamp that covers La Ville Morte comes to life with calls and croaks and chirping. Remind me of New Orleans in a way. After a bit, the captain talks again, though her voice is real low now.

"How long Oya been . . . with you?" she asks.

The question catches me by surprise. Didn't think she wanted to walk down this road again. But I answer. "Long as I know myself. Ma maman said Oya's strong in her people's blood. The womenfolk, anyway." I pause before venturing my own question. "How long Oshun been with you?"

The captain takes a while, then says: "My grandmother see she in me since I was small. We house was near a river." She stops again. "Sometimes, I could hear those waters singing to me sweet, sweet. They call my name. Like they know me."

In my head Oya whispers words that I repeat: "Oshun is at home in the rivers."

The captain makes a face like that's not what she wants to hear. "My grandmother say Oshun can show me secrets in those waters, learn me how to heal and make people love and laugh." She snorts. "But that not what I want to do with my life. I make up my mind that no goddess ruling me. When I big enough I run from that river, away from that sweet song."

I look down at the waters of the swamp. These waters come from Lake Pontchartrain—Oshun's domain. "You hear that song right now?" I ask. There's more silence. Then . . .

"Yes," the captain admits, voice down to a whisper now. "All around me. Calling."

So that explain why the woman is so damned fidgety. Whenever there's a storm or high winds, Oya is at her strongest. I can hear her blaring in my head and all around me. In these waters, Oshun must be like that for the captain. Fighting it has to be like trying to push back a flood. In my head, Oya laughs. You can run from those old Afrikin goddesses. But they find you when they ready.

"You sure you good for what we about to do?" I ask.

"I doing fine," the captain says tightly. "It's nothing."

Her words don't sound convincing.

"If you try not to fight her it won't be as bad," I suggest.

The captain grimaces. "And let she take hold of me?"

"You don't have to if you don't want. Just listen, instead of trying to shut her out."

"I can hear she all over the blasted place!"

"Hearing ain't the same as listening," I counter. She's set to start up again, but I don't let her. "Stop being so stubborn for once! If you don't want to let her in, then don't. But she might have something useful to say!" I pause before saying the next part. "What the sisters said, about you and me, about Oya and Oshun being out here together, might be some truth to that."

The captain frowns and I sigh. Might as well tell all of it.

"The same night this all started, right before I overhear the Cajun and the Confederates in my alcove, I got a vision," I say. "Oya, she sends me them sometimes. About things to come. That night I see a great big moon but like a skull. It swallow up the whole city. I didn't know what it mean until the sisters helped me put it all together. Whatever happening out here, Oya knows and she sent me a warning. Could be Oshun done the same for you."

The captain gives me a long pondering look, then shakes her head. "I don't get no visions." Another long pause. "But sometimes I does feel when something real bad going to happen. Feel it deep, deep inside. Since we come into this Dead City, it come over me strong."

I nod, knowing that kind of thing all too well. "There's a man," I tell her. "Tall in a black suit. I seen him one time on the streets. He was driving the wagon this morning. I think his face—his mask—is the same as the one in my vision. There's something about him." I fumble, not sure how to explain. "Just, be careful around that one."

Féral turns to us suddenly, pressing a finger to her lips for quiet. We've stopped behind a thick knotted oak that's pushing up and through a crumbling moss-stained brick wall. The big tree look odd here among the swamp cypress, probably planted when the city was still alive. But it stay strong, still growing and making this land its own. On the other side of the oak tree, maybe about a carriage car's length from where we crouch, there's a collapsed building that look like it might have been a big plantation house. Now it sits there in a mound of rotted wood and stone jutting up from the waters like a small island. A set of worn rickety shacks are still sitting on a bank of earth, pushed up against each other and covered in moss. I'm guessing they was once slave cabins that somehow survived better than their master's house. There's men standing around there too, dressed in a mismatch of gray and red uniforms. A long strip of cloth hangs from one of the shacks, a tattered thing with a big yellow star in a sea of red, beside red, white, and blue stripes. The old Louisiana Confederate flag. Looks like we found the Jeannots. And that's not all.

The captain taps at me, pointing.

It's the Haitian scientist—right out in the open! Not hard to make him out. He's the only black man in the group. He's stripped down to the blue vest of his suit and wearing a long gray apron that cover him to his ankles. He's giving directions to some Jeannots who are putting what looks like an artillery shell into the biggest cannon I ever seen: a thing of coal-black iron with a barrel long as a rail. They're being real careful with the shell too, stuffing it in with a lengthy pole. When it's done they all step back and four more Jeannots start turning spoked iron wheels on either side of the cannon—two of them at each. A loud squeaking and grinding echoes through the swamp as that black barrel starts to rise, lifting slow, bit by bit, until it's pointing right into the sky—not straight up, but at a high angle. And I know what's just been put in that cannon.

"Shango's Thunder!" I whisper under my breath.

"Blasted man gone and make it for them!" the captain seethes, realizing the same. She turns and gives a set of hand signals to the bearded Haitian and the Mongolian. The two take off immediately, setting out in opposite directions through the drowned city. "Francois and Nogai going to start up one set of noise, make these Jeannots think a whole army coming for them," she explains. "That will get they attention. Then I going to get Duval and smash that damn cannon!"

I eye her doubtfully, counting over a dozen Jeannots. They hear that noise, chances are they gonna grab the scientist and run. But she pulls out her Free Isles pistol with some strange-looking bullets I never seen before. "You and Féral stay here." She stops, her face turning into a frown. "Where that girl gone?"

I look to my side to see Féral's missing. Both of us spin around searching, but there's no sign of the girl. A shout from one of the Jeannots turns us back to their camp. The captain curses. I shake my head. Sure enough, there's Féral.

The girl is striding out the water up to the Jeannots, like she's just out for a Sunday stroll. The first one to spot her was the one to yell out. Now there's at least half of the group running over to surround her. Féral just stands there looking up at them with wide eyes. I didn't even know she could make them that big. The men crowd about, some asking questions. When one of them reaches a hand she darts back. Another one approaches, this time offering what looks like food. Féral snatches it up and begins ramming it into her mouth, then grins wide—setting the men to laughter.

"What is that blasted child doing?" the captain hisses.

I smile as I answer. "Getting their attention." I point to the Haitian scientist, who by now is standing almost by himself. Even his guard's eyes are on Féral. The captain don't waste time. Crouching, she starts forward. I follow—having no intention of being left behind. We creep right up into the Jeannots' camp and the captain gets a hold of the scientist, dragging him to the side of one of the shacks. He don't cry out, just stares at us like he can't believe that he's seeing us.

"You going to come with me," she tells him, "or you going to be dead? Understand?"

The man's eyes swerve to where her pistol is lodged at his chest, but he shakes his head.

"I cannot!" he says through a thick Haitian accent. "Not without my jewel!"

"I don't care what they paying you!" the captain growls, pressing the pistol harder.

But the man keeps shaking his head. And he's crying now. I frown, remembering from when we met him on the street. I seen greedy men and women before. I know how their eyes light up when they talk about riches. There's something about the way he says "jewel," though, that's different. He don't say it like he's talking about money. It's like something more personal.

"Moushay Duval," I ask. "What is this . . . jewel?"

He turns to look at me, and seems momentarily surprised all over again to find himself staring at a girl. But he answers. "My daughter," he says hoarsely.

I exchange a startled glance with the captain. Jewel isn't a thing. It's a name.

"Confederates take her," the man explains, reading our faces. "Make me work for them. I almost had her back. Then these Jeannots come for me and take her too. If I don't give them what they want, they will sell her! Into the Confederacy!"

I grimace. Slave snatching was punishable by death in free New Orleans. But some still did it. You got sold into the Confederate States, and wasn't no coming back.

"Where your daughter now?" the captain asks. The man points to one of the shacks.

"I will not leave without her," he proclaims. "You will have to kill me first!"

His voice is wavering, but I think he means it. I also think the captain just might pull that trigger on him if she has to. "I'll get her," I blurt out quickly. Both of them look to me with startled expressions. "You didn't come here just to kill him," I tell the captain. "And I don't see him coming with us otherwise. We can't all three get back there. So I'll get her. Just wait."

I don't give them a chance to disagree, grabbing onto

and climbing the big oak easy. Like I say, I ain't get this name Creeper for nothing. I pull myself up and onto a long branch, ambling right over a bunch of Jeannots with them being none the wiser. The knotted bough extends above one of the shacks. I follow it along its length and drop down onto the roof, praying the whole while the rotted wood don't give way underneath me. From there, I crouch-walk to the ledge and hang my body over for a look. There's a window, just a cut-out hole with a simple shutter hanging half off its hinges. I can see through a small space and make out a single Jeannot inside: a little squat man who's leaning against a wall looking bored. There's one chair in the room. And tied to it, in front of a table with an oil lamp, is a girl. She look a little older than me, wearing a torn-up yellow dress that might have been nice once and a white scarf tying back her hair. Her eyes stare at the burning lamp, big and frightened.

It's as I'm wondering how I'm going to go about getting her out that the explosion comes.

Boom!

I scramble back onto the roof and look out into the swamp to see a fireball lighting up the dark, making the buildings of the Dead City shimmer like ghosts. Another one goes off on the other side. Boom! Then there's the pat-pat-pat of gunshots, coming from out in the swamp. The Mongolian and the Haitian, I remember. Got the Jeannots running back and forth now like a kicked-over anthill. Probably got them to thinking the whole New Orleans Guard is out there. They start shooting back into the dark, yelling and shouting at what they can't see. None of them know what to make of the canisters that come flying at them. The first one just falls into the waters. The second and third ones though reach the patch of land and send off big clouds of bright green vapor that almost glows in the dark. Drapeto gas!

I remember the gas mask I'm carrying—another gift from the sisters—and strap it on quick, breathing clean air through the filters as I watch the drapeto billowing about. The Jeannots who get a whiff of it start choking, coughing, and rubbing at their eyes while swearing. Then they go dead quiet, standing with their guns held slack at their sides and staring out at nothing. That sends the rest of them into even more disarray, trying to see through the haze of green mist and stumbling over the ones that won't move, all while trying to fight at the same time. I have to admit, it feel good to see the drapeto work on them. But it still makes my skin crawl.

The door to the shack swings open and I duck down quick. It's the Jeannot that was inside. He comes out with a rifle and is swept up by a band of other Jeannots, running out to join the fight. He left the girl alone, unguarded! This the best chance I'll get.

I creep back to the window, stretching and angling my body to open it. With a push the shutter gives way and I swing down, slipping inside. It's just the girl in the shack now. She jumps in the chair and screams at the sight of me, just as another boom goes off. If she was scared before, she's terrified now, and is talking in a stream of Haitian creole I can barely understand. When I move closer, she only screams again. It takes me a minute to realize it's the mask. I undo the straps and pull it off so she can see my face.

"Jewel!" I snap sharply. "Jewel Duval!"

That sends her quiet and she stares at me blankly behind a set of weepy brown eyes.

"I'm here to get you out!" I say, bending down to loosen the ropes about her wrists and ankles. "Your father sent me! You understand?"

She nods but still looks confused, licking a set of parched lips before speaking. "Wi. It is just . . . you?"

I scowl up at her. I happen to think I'm plenty.

"Come on!" I bark, once I've gotten her out of the ropes. "We have to go before they come back! Only got one mask. So get something to wrap your face. You don't want to breathe in what's outside." I rush to the door, pulling it open—to find it blocked. Jeannots. Three of them. Two are armed with rifles. But the guns they holding aren't what makes my stomach feel like it wants to empty. It's the tall skinny man in the middle: the one in a black mortician's suit and wearing that frightful skeleton mask. His blue eyes swivel to glare down at me from behind that skull, and there's the sudden surprise of recognition. I don't give him a chance for more.

I call on Oya. This time, there's no reluctance or fickleness. She's there, bristling and ready to fight. A gust of wind picks up, strong enough to blow all three men out my way. Or at least it should be. It picks up the two armed men right off their feet, sending them spinning into the night. But the tall one in the mask, skinny or no, must be sturdier than the rest. He crouches low down and somehow keeps his footing in the blast of air even as his companions fly away. His head cocks to the side like a crow as he looks me over.

"So you got dem old powers on your side, cher," he remarks almost playfully. "Dat nice. Real nice. Except I got me somethin' to protect from witchery." His hand moves up to pat a small red pouch on a thin cord about his neck. I curse. A mojo bag! How hadn't I seen that before? That explains why he seems so strange. Just my luck to run into a Jeannot who knows some Hoodoo. In my head Oya growls her distaste. She's kind of touchy about the folk magic.

Standing up, the tall man steps into the room and I immediately back away with Jewel clutching behind me.

"Oh don't go nowhere now, cher," he mocks. "Come all this way just to see me. We can get to know each other a little better. Darkeys like a good song and dance, no?" His feet begin an odd sweeping shuffle across the floor as his voice picks up a familiar tune:

> *"If Jackson should be President,*
> *We'll borrow guns of Government,*
> *And you may load and I'll tend vent,*
> *Then touch her off and let her went,*
> *With huzza! For Andrew Jackson!"*

In a blur, he pulls a curved knife from inside his suit and darts right for me.

I jump back. Nobody should be able to move that fast, but he do. Oya's wind is there again, pushing hard against him, so hard the whole cabin shake—and I fear for a moment it might fall in about us. But the man twists his lanky body like a sidewinding river snake, sliding around the gust of air easy as ever.

I'm still backing up, hearing the heels of my boots on the wooden planks, my mind warning me there's soon going to be nowhere to go—and I'll just be trapped in here with him. But there's no time to think as he suddenly bounds forward in one big leap, that curved knife flashing silver in the flickering lamplight like a serpent's fang.

I throw up an arm to protect myself, all I can manage to do to as the blade comes close to slicing my face.

There's a sharp sting, followed soon after by a powerful burning up and down my forearm. I glance to see the sleeve of my coat sliced open, and there's blood soaking through the tear and into the fabric, warm and wet and running down to drip from my fingers. The pain is enough to make me stumble back, lose balance, and slip awkwardly to one knee. The tall man takes his time now, back to doing his shuffling dance and humming his damn tune. Behind me Jewel is shrieking in my ear, and I'm reminded how much I hate to hear folk screaming their fool heads off. What good that going to do? I want to turn and tell her to hush up, to let me think, but my eyes are locked on that skull's face that's coming for me. I don't even think I can move. I feel trapped there and held in place. He's twirling that knife between his fingers, the edge of it red with my blood, grinning his skeleton grin the whole while.

"Come see, cher," he croons, beckoning with a finger. "Don't be scared. Don't run. I just want to cut you open. See what a witch insides made from. Maybe pull them out, and play with them some. I let you watch too." He laughs and does a little hop and slide. "I can't lie to you though, cher. It gonna hurt. It gonna hurt a lot. Real, real bad."

He goes still for a moment—then moves all at once, coming at me quick as a shadow, that blade glinting as it shoots forward. I inhale, bracing for it to bite into me, knowing this time it's gonna dig deep. But my attacker stops short, crying out suddenly instead. Something's latched onto him, a small shape with teeth buried into his knife hand. I blink in surprise. Féral!

I got no idea how the swamp girl got here so fast, but she's there and biting hard. The tall man tries to fling her way but she's holding on tight. She must clamp down even harder or chew or something, because he looses one loud howl of pain and drops the knife. Only then does she let go. He curses, pressing his injured hand to his chest and lashing out to cuff her with the other. But she's too fast—scurrying back and forth and then coming at him again and again, a small fury of wild hair, digging fingernails, and those blessed teeth!

I don't waste time, grabbing up the closest thing to me—the lamp. The eyes in that skeleton mask turn just in time to see it swinging hard for his head. There's a crack once. Twice. Then something big breaks over him, sending a shower of broken and splintered wood flying in every direction. I turn in surprise to see Jewel Duval holding what's left of a chair. She's looking down at the tall man, who's laid out at our feet. Screaming something in Creole she kicks him hard in the head. That grinning skull jerks to one side, flopping like a melon. But he don't move. I smile and she nods back in satisfaction, the anger in her eyes saying she wants to hit him again. Girl got more in her than I thought. With my good hand, I smash what's left of the lamp on the shack floor. Fiery fluid spills out and moves quick across the rotted wood that goes up like kindling.

"We gotta get out now!" I shout. The three of us run, stumble and trip our way from the shack. It's not pretty or graceful, but we get out. The Jeannots barely pay us any mind. The ones with a head full of drapeto just stand there swaying, like strange looking trees. The rest had sense enough to bundle their faces up with whatever they could find. They scamper all around, yelling and carrying on, in a shootout with what they think is an army they still can't see. I let Féral take my mask since she seem to have lost hers. Me and Jewel use torn-away parts of her dress to keep our noses and mouths covered. Not much of the gas left, just faint airy wisps. But I think I can taste it on my tongue—remind me of licking metal. We thread our way between the shacks to where the captain and the Haitian scientist are waiting. There's two crumpled up Jeannots laying in a heap who must have come look-ing for the man—either unconscious our dead, I don't bother to check too close.

Doctor Duval cries out when he sees his daughter, ripping off a mask he'd been given before grabbing and hugging her tight. The captain seizes me, inspecting the gash on my arm, her eyes showing concern behind her mask. But I snatch it back. Hurts a whole lot, yes. But it seems least important right now. A shout from the Jeannots says they've noticed the fire I started, which is eating up that one shack and starting to spread. We stay here and they'll find us soon enough.

"How we getting out all this?" I ask the captain, pulling down the cloth from my face.

She lifts off her own mask, sniffing and testing the air until she's satisfied it's safe. She sends another frown at my arm, but answers my question by lifting her pistol to the air and firing. There's the clap of a gunshot that's loud enough to tell everyone our position. And I think maybe she's gone crazy. But instead of a bullet there's a stream of smoke trailing from the barrel—like the fireworks I seen on Free New Orleans Day celebrations and the like. It flies high then explodes in a burst of bright colours against the black night. The captain searches the sky as the lights die out, looking hard for something.

"Come on, come on!" she mutters tight, almost under breath. "Bring my doux-doux darling to me. Blast your eyes, allyuh have to see that! Follow it!"

I follow her gaze to the sky, not understanding. Bring what to her? Who had to see? I'm still wondering when my ears catch a sound: a deep familiar hum. It grows louder by the moment, like it's getting closer. My eyes widen as I realize where I've heard that sound before, up in my alcove on Les Grand Murs. It's the sound of spinning ship propellers. Suddenly there's light. It's blinding. I cover my eyes, blinking until I can see. And I make out the incredible sight of an airship! Lord almighty! It's big and beautiful, hanging right over the Dead City, its lamps searching about the swamp before training down on us. In the glare, I can just read the words painted in big gold letters on its hull—*Midnight Robber.*

The captain grins. "We ride reach!"

The Jeannots spin about, shocked so much at first they barely move. And there's this long stretch of quiet, except for those spinning propellers. Then one of them lets out that banshee yell they so famous for and starts shooting into the air. The rest join in, yipping and hollering and aiming all their fire on the airship. But that thing's got guns too—bigger guns. When they shoot back it sound like loud handclaps one right after the other, and bullets rain down on the Jeannots with the force of a hammer. It tear through knots of them at a time. The ones still swaying with drapeto don't even cry out when they're hit. They just fall into the swamp, quiet. It don't take long before the rest of them break and run for cover. Some even drop their rifles, scrambling fast as their feet can carry them deeper into the swamp. I laugh at the sight. They ain't yipping and hollering now! The *Midnight Robber* makes a sweep above the city that clears the whole area, then comes to hover right above us. A rope ladder with iron rungs falls out, and hanging at its end is the Hindoo—looking pretty as ever. He smiles and I stifle the blushing again, though his eyes are all for the captain.

"Need some assistance, my lady?" he calls out dramatically.

"Ravi!" she greets with a whoop.

So it's Ravi then, is it? I decide to remember that name.

"You could have mentioned you were bringing a whole airship," I comment.

The captain shoots me a crooked grin. "Had to time it right. If it didn't work, all now so we running back to New Orleans!" She turns back to Ravi, who's standing now beside us. Her hand motions to me, Féral, Doctor Duval, and his daughter. "See about getting all ah them on the ship! François and Nogai should be making their way back. The three of we going to—"

She don't get to finish before the boom goes off. It's so loud I jump. The ground shakes beneath our feet, leaving us all rattled and my ears ringing. Another explosion, I wonder? No, more than that, I realize, feeling a chill creep along my skin. I turn toward the cannon, where white smoke is curling up out from the rounded black muzzle.

"No!" I breathe out, not wanting to accept what I'm seeing.

The captain is already running for the cannon and I follow close behind. When we reach it, you can smell the stink of the gunpowder thick in the air: sour and bitter all at once. There's a Jeannot lying on the ground. I gasp at the sight of him. It's the tall man in the black suit! I was certain I left him for dead in that shack, but no mistaking that's him! He look bad off. His clothes are almost all burnt away and his mask is melted on one side, showing scorched blistered skin underneath. But damn if he ain't still alive! Just my luck he didn't go up in the fire. Don't even know how he managed to crawl out here in all this confusion. But he's here now, sprawled out with one arm extended. I follow it to where his hand is clutching at a long wire that extends back to the cannon. I seen those before. They what you pull to make a cannon fire. And I know then what he's done.

He begins to cough and laugh at the same time and from under his breath I can hear him croaking out a song:

> "'Twas when they let a cannon fly,
> Then up went rockets in the sky,
> Huzza! For Jackson was the cry . . ."

He chokes and stops, angling those icy blue eyes to fix

on me. I'm expecting him to curse or spit. But instead he smiles wide—showing half real yellowed teeth and half a melted white mask. "Looks like I win, cher," he rasps feebly. "Here come . . . death." His head turns away to rest facing up, eyes staring as a slow hiss escapes from that unchanging grin and he goes still.

I follow his gaze to where the cannon shell has exploded in the night sky—a big puff of gray smoke spreading out in every direction. It reminds me of a storm cloud, though growing and moving different from any I ever seen. Not too hard to figure out what it is: Shango's Thunder.

Doctor Duval runs up beside us, his eyes glaring up at that strange expanding cloud.

"We must leave here!" he cries.

The captain is staring up too. "Maybe it won't reach high enough," she says. But her voice don't sound like she believes it. She turns to look at me. And for the first time since we met, I see fright on her face. That scares me even more.

Doctor Duval shakes his head. "Does not matter! The compound, it rises! Even now, it seeds the sky!"

He don't have to tell me. In my head, Oya is chanting louder by the minute. And the air around me is changing. I can feel it, like little needles pricking sharp on my skin. There's a fresh smell like tilled up earth in the air: the kind you get right before a rainstorm. Only this is so strong it's almost overwhelming, filling up my nose and mouth 'til I can taste it. A wind picks up from nowhere. It ripples across the Dead City, whistling between empty streets and corridors, swaying the hanging moss on cypress trees and sending the old buildings to rattling and creaking, so it feel they might topple over. It passes over us in a rush and I shiver as Oya drinks it in. The waters of the swamp are moving too, the wind got it jumping up and down like that pot of gumbo Sister Eunice was cooking—as if somebody set it to boiling. From somewhere up above comes the first deep rumble of thunder, slow and building.

"No!" the captain protests, as if that alone can stop what's coming. There's anguish in her voice. But her eyes aren't on the approaching storm. She's staring out into the distance. Though we can't see it from here, I know she's looking out to New Orleans. The thought makes my heart drop.

"We must go!" Doctor Duval urges again. "There's no more we can do!"

The wind's gotten stronger by now, so that it's howling in our ears.

"He's right!" Ravi shouts coming up. The Haitian and the Mongolian are there at his side, all of them looking worriedly at the sky. "We can't stay here!" he says, nodding towards the *Midnight Robber*. "We get caught up there in this storm, we might not make it out!" The captain still seems reluctant, but she turns and begins giving orders to get back to the airship.

Me, I don't move. My eyes are still fixed on the distance. Oya's vision flickers in my head, its meaning made plain now. The grinning skull rising like a moon over New Orleans is this dead Jeannot at my feet, who's loosed Shango's Thunder on the city. People will be out tonight for the Maddi grá. None of them know what's coming. Nobody even warned them. And now it's too late. This isn't storm season. There are no shelters open. No one's ready for this. Even if the walls hold, whole place will drown in all that rain and wind. Everyone will drown. I can't let that happen, I know at once. Not to my city. I feel a growing anger building up in me. I *won't* let that happen.

The captain sees me standing there and she turns back from the others. The wind is howling louder now as flashes of lightning streak across the night, giving glimpses of dark churning clouds. When the rain starts, it don't fall in drops. It comes in sheets that slants and stings your skin when it hits. The water in the swamp is churning up too, picked up by the wind and crashing against the buildings of the Dead City in waves.

"I'm not going!" I yell, before she can begin. "I have to stop this!"

She stares at me like I've lost my mind. And maybe I have. "How you mean?" she shouts, wiping rain from her face.

"Oya!" I cry back over the rising wind. "I have to get her to help! She can stop this!"

The captain eyes me like she's unsure. "Will she listen to you?"

Lord, I hope so. I close my eyes and call to her. She talks back.

In my head Oya is like a beating drum. I see through her eyes, her memories. I see that day the Frenchies tried to take back Haiti. I see Napoleon's ships like little toy boats to her, tossed along the waves, the wind tearing those big white sails like paper. I see masts and hulls broken to splinters and dashed over the dark waters. Men in blue and white uniforms and bright plumed hats scream as the water fills up their mouths and chests, pulling them down, down, down into the black deep. But that wasn't all. The goddess, she remembers the rest. And it's painful to watch.

I see the storm heave itself from the sea onto land, like a great monster of wind and rain and sea. I see the Haitian soldiers cheering the end of the Frenchies going quiet one by one, watching what's coming for them. Some start to run. But they can't escape this. Now they screaming too. The wind rips through them, flinging people into the air like dolls. The water comes with it, more water than I ever seen: washing away trees and buildings, mashing them all up together and rolling over everyone and everything in its way. The people run. They scream. Some fall to their knees and throw up their hands in prayer. They cry out to their gods to save them. The gods who had helped them win their freedom. They cry out even as the storm swallows them up and delivers them back out to the sea.

Oya remembers it all too well. It wasn't just the Frenchies that got swept away that day. It was her people too. Her people who had brought her with them in the belly of slave ships. Who had sung her songs and made her offerings in this strange new land, calling her by new names and mixing her up with new gods. Her people who had kept her alive, passing on her tales to those who came after. She hadn't meant to harm them. But she was Oya, the rain that grows your crops and the tornado that tears your home apart; the wind that brings change and the storm that reaps destruction. Calling on her was always like flipping a coin: one side a blessing, the other chaos. I'm throwing up that coin now, and praying it comes down on the right side.

"Your people need you now!" I plead. "Just like they did back then. They asked you to be a weapon. And you were as terrible as they wanted you to be. Because that's what we do, isn't it? We change you gods wherever we bring you, make you into whatever we need. You couldn't help your people that got caught in your whirlwind. You couldn't save them in time. But you can save your people now. The ones right here in this city. They remember you, even if they don't always call you by name. They sing and dance your songs. They carry you with them in their stories and memories. I carry you. And we need your protection!"

Oya answers my call with a great shout, filling me up with her power. Hard to explain that feeling. It's like a whole hurricane is swirling up inside me. Like I got lightning at my fingertips and thunder rolling behind my eyes. I can hear drums pounding out a rhythm first played back in old Lafrik, joined in by a rattle and chanting voices. It make my feet want to dance and it seem like the whole world is moving with me. I surrender to it fully, letting the goddess ride me, guide me as her own. I raise up my hands to the storm—her hands too, now. Our hands. The storm roars back, angry, like a child at its mother, trying to make me kneel. But I laugh. I am the Mistress of Winds! I gather them up, forcing them to bend to me. They struggle but I hold on tight, letting Oya work through me, with me, together.

Then something slams me hard. A wave so big it knocks me down. I barely have time to think as my world is turned sideways. I plunge into the rising water of the swamp and am swept away, tossed about and carried along in all that turbulence. My feet slip once, twice on the ground beneath. Then there's no more ground and I'm fighting to swim. But the water's strong: a living thing that wraps around me, pulling me under. I'm sinking now, caught by jutting tree roots and the buried wreckage of a lifeless city. It feels like hands dragging me down. I open my mouth stupidly to cry out and the water rushes in. I can't breathe. And I'm trying to reach up, to find the air and wind that is Oya's domain again. But these waters got me held fast. And I must have hit one of those deep parts, because I feel like I keep going down. Down. Down. Down. Like those Frenchies. Going on to Yemoja's realm. I wonder if, when I get to the bottom, I'll meet them.

Suddenly someone has me. No, not someone. These aren't hands holding onto me. It's the water itself. The very same one that was trying to drown me. But now it's different. Now it's pushing on me, pulling on me, lifting me up. I break the surface, sucking in air and wind by the mouthful. I think it's the sweetest thing I ever tasted. Then I see who it was that saved me.

It's the captain. She's standing in the rising waters of the Dead City. No, she ain't standing in the waters. Lord almighty, she's standing on *top* of the waters! Her head is tilted back and her arms are held wide. She's moving them back and forth like she's doing some kind of dance. And the waters shift with her, great big waves swirling in time to her movements, parting and pushing back to leave a space for both of us. Not just the captain I know. Not just Ann-Marie. Because she's all light again. Golden, beautiful light like the sun breaking through a storm. Oshun, the Bright Lady.

What are the chances that both Oya and Oshun come to New Orleans in both of us at the same time, those two odd nuns had asked? Now I know the answer. No chance. Not chance at all. My sister done her part. Time to do mine.

I rise back up with my hands to the sky, still coughing out water. The storm resists, but I am Oya now. My burgundy dress flows about me as I dance, a machete over my head, in the middle of the whirlwind. I bend those winds to me, making them surrender to my control. I reach up to pluck away bright cords of lightning from the heavens, shaping them in my palm until they're just sparkling bits of fireflies. I plunge fingers into black clouds, swirling them from within until they're untroubled, and a heavy rain turns into a light shower. I laugh as I go about my work. And beside me, my sister Oshun shines.

~

It's a long time after sunrise as I sit on the deck of the *Midnight Robber* looking out at the city. It's Maddi grá morning. I can hear the noise of it faintly—horns and music and people—even now, way up here at the air docks on one of Les Grand Murs. Don't remember much about last night. I woke up here on the *Midnight Robber*. The pretty Hindoo man, Ravi, he say they thought they'd lost the captain and me for good. The airship had been forced to sail away, or it might have been struck right out of the sky. Then the storm stopped suddenly so they could swing back and land again. They found the two of us lying in the swamp—on a dry patch of land where the waters had all pulled back. Thought we was dead, but we were both just passed out. The big Mongolian carried us to the ship slung over his shoulders, he said. Was him that sewed up the gash on my arm. And we'd slept right through until the dawn.

"Glad to see you awake," someone greets me.

I turn to look up at the captain. She's dressed in her Free Isles jacket, standing there straight-backed, bright eyed and rested—appearing every bit the commander of this airship. I watch as she runs a hand along a railing, stroking it like the vessel is alive and can feel her touch. Think I hear her mutter *my doux-doux darling* under her breath.

"Long night," I answer back.

"Damn long," she agrees and sits down with me on her deck, stretching her legs out. For a while we both don't do any talking. It's enough just to take in the sun and the breeze on our faces. Finally, I work up the courage to say what we both avoiding.

"You remember any of what happened?"

The captain takes a while, then shakes her head. "Not too much. But I think...." Her words trail off before she starts up again. "I think I was someone else for a while."

I shake my head back at her. "You were you. Just Oshun too. Thank you for saving me. Thank you for helping save the city."

She gives an uncomfortable shrug. "When you get pulled away by the waters and I couldn't find you, I remember wanting to get you out of there so bad I . . ."

"You opened yourself up," I finish. "You let Oshun in. How was it?"

The captain looks ready to answer. But instead she frowns and straightens, remembering who she is. Within moments her usual stiff face is on.

"About our bargain," she begins.

"You promised to let me be crew," I interject.

"No," she corrects flatly. "I say I will *think* on it. You believe I doesn't know my own mind?"

I fold my arms. It was worth a try. "So? What now?"

"So," she repeats, "what I say before hold true: you too young to be on any airship." Her face is set like a mask that won't give. But then, to my surprise, it softens. "Still, you show me you not just any, any girl. Might be smarter and braver than most grown women I know."

I can't help smiling at the compliment, even if I feel silly doing so.

"But grown women should know their writings and their maths!" she goes on, that firm mask coming back. "And I not going to have any dotish girl on my ship! So, I write a letter to those two obeah women who call themselves nuns. You going to start attending school at the convent." I make a face, ready to gripe at this, but she holds up a hand. "Madame Diouf going to make a donation to them that should take care of you. I see to that myself, for your mother sake. You going to stop sleeping on the blasted streets like a vagrant. And you going to stop stealing. It's damn immoral!"

"You're a smuggler!" I point out, extending my arms to take in the airship.

"But not a thief!" she retorts evenly.

"The name of your ship is *Midnight Robber*!"

She pauses at this. Shrugs. Then says evenly: "It's satire."

I open my mouth to ask what that's supposed to mean, but don't bother. She'd probably just say I needed schooling again. I'm ready to catch a fit at the list of rules. But truth is, my heart isn't in the fight. After last night, I've come to realize just how much I'm attached to this city. Not so sure anymore if I'm ready to leave it just yet. Don't know if Oya's ready either. So, maybe I can bide my time at the convent. The nuns can't be so bad. There'll be plenty of food. And a warm bed. Might be the two will even let me take part in their odd dealings. Maybe I can do something about Féral's hair. I won't miss stealing—much. Though I'll probably sneak out every now and then to my old spot up here, just to look out. Definitely not wearing any frilly dresses, ever!

I nod to accept our arrangement and hold out my hand like I seen gentlemen do when they make a deal. The captain arches an eyebrow but puts out her own hand for one firm shake. I give a sharp yelp. She squeezes hard! Is that how handshakes go? Why would men do that to each other? When it's done, we sit back again.

"What about Doctor Duval and his daughter?" I ask.

"We have them below," the captain replies. "And guarded."

"Will he be in trouble? For what he did?"

The way her face sets, I'm thinking the doctor is in for a world of trouble. But she only says: "Not for me to decide."

Fair enough. "And the drapeto?" I ask. The captain

gives me a blank gaze and I stare back at her plainly. "The sisters gave you four canisters. One went into the swamp. Two blew up. I never saw the fourth." Did the woman really think I didn't notice?

She don't answer me, but there's that impressed look on her face that annoyingly makes me blush inside. "We sailing to Port-au-Prince today," she says instead.

"Today?" That puts thoughts of drapeto and all else out my mind. I'm kind of disappointed to see them go. "You'll miss the Maddi grá!"

The captain shrugs. "It'll be here next year. I'll see it then."

Good, I think. The thought of seeing her again next year is something to look forward to.

"When you come back, I'll show you around," I offer. "You ain't even got to see any of the fancy krewes. Or the second-line parades put on by the colored benevolent societies with their brass bands. Best dancing and music in the city."

"Alright then, Jacqueline," she accepts. "Maybe one day I take you to see Carnival in Trinidad. It bigger even than your Maddi grá."

I almost laugh. Bigger than Maddi grá? I doubt that.

I don't reprimand her for not using my nickname. Not this time. We both turn to look out on the city. Free New Orleans, who don't know how close it came to destruction. Who gets to breathe just a little while longer with no storms on the horizon. Somewhere in my thoughts, Oya starts up humming a song. I think I can hear Oshun join in.

Acknowledgments

Lots of people helped in making and inspiring this story—in more ways than I can count. Thanks to everyone who saw this tale through from spark to finish: Kirk Johnson, for listening to me babble on about worlds I've created and never once saying "shut up already;" Christee Thompson Lewis, who was one of the first to read this story and gave her hometown perspective; Nzinga "Oyaniyi" Metzger, who painstakingly took me through the Black Gods that lay at the heart of this tale; Justina Ireland, who offered her advice and encouragement; Chaz Pitts-Kyser, my long-time muse who goes over every story with a fine-toothed comb; and Diana M. Pho, who took a chance on this story and urged me to make it "more." I want to thank the copy editor and proofreader ahead of time—you guys are magical creatures from Fillory or something, I'm certain. Thanks to my sister, Lisa, who always believed I could do this writing thing. The warmest of thanks goes to my wife, Danielle, for all the love and support.

And finally, thanks to Marcus, who first took me to Bayou Classic back in college—and introduced me to the wonder, cultures, and magic of the Crescent City. Thanks also to NOPD who pressed a loaded pistol to the back of my head as I lay facedown on a posh French Quarter hotel floor in a case of "mistaken identity"—you introduced me to the city too.

To the Creepers out there—keep climbing.

About the Author

Born in New York and raised mostly in Houston, **P. DJÈLÍ CLARK** spent the formative years of his life in the homeland of his parents, Trinidad and Tobago. His writing has appeared in *Daily Science Fiction, Heroic Fantasy Quarterly, Lightspeed, Tor.com,* and print anthologies including *Griots* I and II, *Steamfunk, Myriad Lands Volume 2,* and *Hidden Youth.* He currently resides in a small castle in Hartford, Connecticut, with his wife, Danielle, and a rambunctious Boston terrier named Beres.

pdjeliclark.wordpress.com

twitter.com/pdjeliclark

TOR·COM

Science fiction. Fantasy. The universe.

And related subjects.

*

More than just a publisher's website, *Tor.com*

is a venue for **original fiction, comics,** and

discussion of the entire field of SF and fantasy,

in all media and from all sources. Visit our site

today — and join the conversation yourself.